FLAMING VENGEANCE

The Frost Fervor Concordance Book Two

TOM HANSEN

IceBlazer
Entertainment

Flaming Vengeance

For all those who were inscribed.

Sometimes good comes through adversity. I would not be who I am today had it not been for the internment, and I like who I am.

— RUTH ASAWA

Prologue

Imryll Farora, Frost Queen of the North, paced in front of her large stone desk. Each boot clicked on the marble floor in perfect time to her short-legged steps.

She re-read the report for the fourth time.

In the doorway to her spacious office, Khatar waited, keeping his eyes diverted just enough to not stare at the body on the ground.

She paused, re-reading something from the report. Icy rage crept up her spine and into her neck, spreading out across her scalp and making her white hair stand on end.

"Dammit!"

She kicked the messenger's corpse once again. This time, her magic surged through her, freezing the soldier's limp flesh where her foot connected.

The man's forearm shattered, hurling icy chunks across the floor.

Khatar shifted from one leg to another, it was a minute change, but she noticed.

She dared him to cringe, dared him to make even the slightest noise. She needed another excuse to take out her rage.

Today was not a good day.

Initial reports from the Feond front spoke of nothing but rough terrain, harsh conditions, and magic that confounded her best wizards. Already, ten percent of her troops had been lost due to circumstances not related to the main task.

How difficult was it to climb up a mountain to place foci along the peak?

She wanted to head out there herself to take care of the issue, but doing so meant she wouldn't be here when her next project arrived.

Imryll couldn't leave right now, not when things were finally coming into place. In a few months, yes, but not until she completed an important task.

For now, she needed to rely on her soldiers to prepare for her arrival. With any luck, they would get back on task and complete it by the time she was ready.

Movement out the window caught Imryll's attention. She glanced out over the edge toward the massive cliff face. Far below, a rider left the main gate, clad all in black.

Captain Nora had taken her punishment like the obedient soldier she was. Imryll was grateful for that. No one had heard from the other Skarmyord, the one in white, for a couple weeks now, ever since they'd lost the two red-haired sisters.

She watched Nora ride until the white flurries blocked her vision.

There was something calming about watching her soldiers ride off into the storm to carry out her bidding. Her anger cooled, Imryll finally looked at her assistant.

"Khatar, what do you have for me?"

The assistant bowed, still not meeting her gaze. "News from Reyoarfjell, Your Majesty."

"Reyoarfjell?" She'd been waiting on the report. It had been too long since any real progress was made.

He bowed, his long black hair reaching down to the ground and almost skimming the surface. "Progress has improved, Your Majesty. For the first time he has managed to keep one alive. It took some doing, but there were no catastrophic failures this time. Unfortunately, the subject's mind was too far gone that it would be near-unusable in the field, but the body handled it fine."

"Catastrophic failures, huh?"

Khatar nodded.

She huffed, tapping a long fingernail on the stony desktop. "Have you ever noticed that scientists never seem to come out and say what they mean? They couch everything in what-ifs and double speak so they have an out if things don't turn out the way they expect."

Imryll spun, walking to the side of the room for her bookshelf. Her boots clicked on the marble floors with a pleasing echo. She loved the sound. It reminded her of an age long ago when life was simpler. An age when her place in the world was expected, even admired. Now she had to fight for every inch of respect in this harsh, unforgiving landscape.

Imryll frowned, pushing the ancient thoughts from her head.

"So you mean the subject is still alive after everything?"

Khatar returned a half smile. "Yes, Your Majesty, and somewhat controllable, but only barely. I believe he compared it to a starving frost bear."

She raised her eyebrows, her mind latching on to the

thought and thinking of the possibilities. "We can control starving frost bears."

He nodded. "Of course, Your Majesty."

This was better news than she expected. It almost made her smile.

"Thank you, Khatar. I would like some tea."

He didn't move.

Icy fury chilled her veins for a split second before she halted the unconscious reaction. It wouldn't do to kill every servant for insubordination.

Besides, he saw her naked nearly every day. Men like that were hard to find anymore.

"Did you have something else, Khatar?"

He bowed his head to the side in deference. "Yes, My Lady. The two sisters finished processing, and while details haven't been sent, the testing showed unparalleled abilities of the highest magnitude imaginable. Testing has been reprioritized over the next week to provide more detail. They will send an updated status as soon as they have more concrete information."

Imryll took a couple careful steps, giving herself much-needed time to process all this information.

"This is good, this is very good."

"Yes, My Lady. Shall I get you that tea now?"

"Yes, I also want you to draw a bath." She looked down at her robe, coated with the soldiers frozen blood. "I'm a bit messy and would like to properly celebrate this new information."

Khatar bowed low once again. "Of course, My Lady. I will tidy up your office while you bathe."

With that, he was gone, like a shadow's whisper.

Maybe that was the reason she enjoyed her metal-covered

boots so much. She liked the noise, the metallic *click click click* as she moved about her day. Everything else in her life was ghostly servants and the ever-present howl of the northern winds.

It wasn't a litany of harp music, but it would have to do.

Imryll sat down and stared out over the valley once again. Adjusting her vision allowed her to see the Feond in the distance.

The shimmer glared at her, and she grinned back.

This was very good news. So very good.

Chapter One

Ynya Oblique squinted as she waited for her sister's signal. It had been too long since they had made contact and Ynya was beginning to get worried.

She wished Synol had the same ability to flash her hair, but a flint and steel turned out to be an effective, albeit more noisy, alternative.

In the darkness, she monitored more than one form move about the small rise. Both road patrols wandered their posts, stamping their feet to try to keep out the cold and keep themselves awake.

A flash of light the next hill over caught her attention. A second later, the light flashed once again.

This time, Ynya focused on it. Synol's bright red hair and serious face was just visible against the dark night sky.

There she is.

It was about time. Ynya was getting tired. Lately, the soldiers had been posting so many sentries at night that wasn't until the sun was about to come up that the sisters were able to make their move.

Ynya had stopped counting out a delay two days ago.

None of it mattered, anyway. Synol wouldn't act until Ynya had gone down there anyway, so why bother counting to the second if you're still waiting on your partner to do the work?

That's probably good enough.

Ynya shrugged off her leather bag, noting the location next to the scraggly pine tree to the north of the camp. She put up the hood on her stolen soldier's uniform and buttoned up the front.

She looked in the bag, a gift from Miss-Miss who had insisted on giving her something smaller to carry things.

It turned out to be quite handy to have everything she needed right there. The cross-body strap held things securely and kept things conveniently at her hip instead of on her back.

She hated this part, the smelly clothes, the subterfuge, the idle chit chat as she pretended to be a soldier. She wished Synol would just do it, she was always better with the subtleties of language and knowing what to say.

I just want to blow shit up.

Ynya stood and jogged down slope to the soldier in the road. Given how cold things were out here and the constant howling of the wind from the east, she easily got within a few paces of him before he noticed her.

She raised her hand at him.

"It's your lucky day."

The soldier chuckled. "Oh yeah, how so?"

"Well," Ynya pulled the hood back on her large winter coat. "I'm here to save your life, but only if you can answer me one question."

His eyes widened, seeing her mass of curly red hair bounce out of the hood and catch in the wind.

He took a step back, still trying to process the sudden arrival of the largest threat to any soldier in the Hyndalskyr district.

He dropped to his knees. "I'll do whatever it takes, just please don't hurt me. I'm not a mage, I've never been to Reyoarfjell, I was just conscripted into the army and told that if I didn't do what they said, my wife and kids would be killed."

She stopped walking toward him and let her hands fall to her side. She smiled. "That is actually the answer I was looking for. Where are you from?"

"Laugar, to the south, Ma'am."

She chuckled, "Ma'am was what people called my mother."

"Sorry, Miss."

She frowned. "I'm not sure that's any better, but it is no matter. "Can you make it to Holmslatr on your own if you leave right now?"

He glanced toward the south-west. "Holmslatr? Isn't Lyraville–"

She shook her head, cutting him off. "Lyraville might not be around by tomorrow."

Horrified understanding swept across his face and his eyes went wide as he looked back toward the east. "I...I...yes, I can make it."

"What about the rest of the contingent? How many are loyal to the Frost Queen?"

"Just the captain and one other man, the big guy with the bald head. We call him The Cobbler."

Ynya nodded. "I suggest you head for Holmslatr now and get to a safe distance, but wait for any other soldiers to catch up. Whatever you do, do not go to Marsfjord. Huddle up for warmth, make it to Holmslatr. If you arrive with your arms up and mention that you abandoned the army, you will be welcomed there, but your name and number will be logged in case we see you in the army again. You only get this one chance to return to your family."

He nodded. "Thank you, Ma'am."

"It's time for me to handle this Cobbler fella. You said big guy?"

"Yes, big guy, shaved head."

Ynya grunted.

She grabbed a single strand of hair from her head to hold between her fingers. She flashed three quick lights, followed by two more.

Synol replied a few seconds later with a spark from her flint.

"As you can see, we're more than prepared for this, so head on out and make sure to help anyone else that comes along here in about an hour."

With that, the man took off into the snow.

Chapter Two

Y nya shrugged off the soldier's coat and pants so it was very clear who she was. Bright red dress, bright red hair, pale skin. If anyone had any doubt who she was at this point, she would make them understand.

She padded into the camp on the balls of her feet, softly melting the packed frost below her feet before they crunched anything.

Her body brimmed with power, having consumed a sizable amount of food this morning. They had run out of fish the night before, but a vegetarian diet from Synol made life bearable. The two complemented each other when it came to survival. Ynya kept their hideouts and the ground warm enough for Synol, who used her magic to grow an incredible array of foods. Ynya then cooked them all to perfection and they feasted like queens.

Stopping back in Marsfjord, Synol had retrieved an array of seeds that their mother kept safe, thus giving them even more variety of foods to eat.

Ynya had even tried her hand at boiling water and cooking some of the potatoes, which turned out to be a favorite of theirs when turned into a creamy soup.

Once in position behind the larger tent, Ynya blinked her hair once, and waited.

This was always the most exciting part.

The rumbling started immediately. With every casting, Synol became more precise in her wall placement, and faster with her delivery of whatever magical gas was deep underground in what Synol called pockets.

Ynya wasn't sure how the earth had pockets, but whatever.

The upheaved stone threw Ynya into air.

All around the camp, rocks vaulted into the sky, blocking off any route from escaping.

The men in the camp scrambled.

Shouts of terror were drowned out by the massive ground quake that shook the entire area. Ynya had heard it all before.

Silence. A complete ring of stones surrounded the campsite, with Ynya standing atop one of them.

"So you're the bitch who keeps killing off my men." A man stood in the center. He wasn't very tall, but he had the air of superiority that marked him for a trained soldier in the Queen's army.

"You have me mistaken for another girl in a red dress with red hair, Sir. I have not killed any of your soldiers tonight, I can assure you."

Around the camp, the dozen or so soldiers huddled together, unsure if they should stay toward the middle or huddle near the end. Off to one side, a man tried to cover himself with blankets and wrap himself in a tent, mumbling incessantly about not wanting to die.

"That may be, but you are wanted for high treason from Her Majesty and we're here to bring you in."

Ynya frowned, stepping from one rock to the other. She stood at least a dozen feet off the ground compared to the men below. "I have the high ground, I decide which of these stones goes down, and I also control how much flame will consume this area."

To punctuate her point, she snapped her fingers. A small flame erupted between her thumb and forefinger. She held it for a second before snuffing it out.

It was a trick, of course. Her heat abilities didn't allow her to hold live fire like some other fire mages did. Synol had the idea to keep some candle wax on her fingertips after watching Ynya light candles one night.

It was long enough that she melted the wax and it burned for a few seconds. It wasn't the same as a fireball, but it was enough to fool anyone they'd met up to this point.

As-expected, the campsite filled with terrified cries and wails of anguish.

"Men, hold fast. We know something the witch doesn't."

She took another step to the side. "Oh, and what's that?"

"That we brought our own mage."

The ground below Ynya fell. She followed a heartbeat later.

She had just enough time to turn her body in the direction of Synol, trying to figure out why her sister had pulled the rock out from under her.

But what she saw was not good.

Atop the small hill by the camp, a burly bald man held up Synol by her throat.

Ynya hit the ground hard. The fall was as painful as it was

unexpected. She felt her ribs crack as she hit the frozen surface, and pain lanced through her chest and fanned through her back.

Her left arm hurt too, possibly cracked. It was a good thing she was so light, otherwise she would have most likely broken more bones.

She was on her feet in an instant. Soldiers to one side, her sister to the other.

Ynya felt every heartbeat as she weighed her options on which way to run. Should she go for Synol and take out the mage, or should she go for the captain and rally the soldiers behind her cause?

Time raced by as she calculated out her options. Her sister or the captain?

That was an easy answer.

She turned toward the hill and sprinted through the snow. Her sister came first, every time. If there was one lesson she had learned recently, it was that family was the correct answer. Besides, most of the soldiers in the rock would scatter rather than stand and fight.

The sun peeked over the horizon, bathing their battleground in fresh light. Ynya focused on her sister's dark-purple face.

Something thudded into her ass. She ignored the pain.

Shouts and commands followed Ynya up the slope as the captain rallied his men to follow her.

Another arrow narrowly missed her, *thunking* into the ground to her left.

Good, at least he's not another Skarmyord.

Ynya needed three more steps to get to Synol. Her hands were already pouring massive heat into her fingernails as she leapt at the man holding her sister.

For a split second as she sailed through the air, she marveled at how long she'd grown her fingernails and meticulously filed them to points in order to allow them to dig into the man's chest easier.

Not that the red-hot nails needed any help.

Chapter Three

Synol practically spat at her sister. "Why do you always have to be such a hero when it comes to life and death situations?"

Ynya turned around. "I know you keep insisting that you had that guy, but he had you around the throat and your face was deep purple. What should I have thought?"

Synol huffed. "You should have let me handle it. Just because he was controlling my magic didn't mean I couldn't. I was waiting for the right time to use it. You did notice that I had the wall of the camp sealed back up by the time you finished killing him?"

Ynya picked up her pack and slung it over her shoulder. Her broken ribs ached something terrible, but there wasn't any way to heal them right now. They would mend in time. Luckily, nothing else seemed to break. Her wrist was sore, but something about burning a man's heart in his chest just made her feel like there was something right in the chaotic world.

In the distance, the last of the soldiers seeking freedom disappeared over the horizon.

Ynya adjusted the pack around her shoulder to stop it from bouncing against her ribs. "I did notice it, but I assumed you did that after I was dealing with your little problem. Besides, if you are going wait around all that time, you could have at least clued me in so that I would have gone after the captain first."

Synol grabbed the bridge of her nose. She closed her eyes and let out a long, careful breath. "Ynya–"

"Don't 'Ynya' me. I know all the lectures, alright? Can we just deal with this last man? It's been a week and I don't know what is going on with Finny and Meki. I don't want to argue about past things. I just want us to work together and get them back safe. Anything other than that isn't worth our time."

Ynya tromped through the snow after the restrained captain, whose voice had gone hoarse at least half an hour before and hadn't quieted down even under threat of Ynya burning his tongue out.

Synol had told her that was out of the question, in front of him.

Aargh! She's so frustrating!

"Ynya, I'm sorry. I just...I just forgot how headstrong both of us can be. You were right, I should have signaled you better, but I just ask that you take a second to assess your situation before reacting to everything with anger and fire."

Ynya fought the urge to turn and scream at her sister. She tried to get along, despite Synol's insistence to talk about every little problem that sprang up between them.

"I'll have you know I spent plenty of time assessing the situation. The captain was behind me, surrounded by terrified soldiers, you were up the hill, purple as an saxifrage with your arms flailing wildly around you. The man holding you grinned like he was a dog who'd caught his first bird and didn't know quite what to do with it. Do I need to go on? I do think things through. I'm sorry if I just process things faster than you, but I looked at the entire situation and made a decision. I think I made the right decision and I'm sorry if your safety is higher on my priority list than the Frost Queen's army, but I will choose my family every time over anything else."

Ynya clomped a few more paces through the snow before she realized Synol wasn't right behind her. She turned.

Synol stood there, a big dumb grin on her face. The sunlight behind her filled her long red hair with a brilliance Ynya hadn't seen in many women.

She looked so much like her mother in that moment that Ynya's breath hitched.

Mama had always told Ynya that she was a spitfire and as cute as a snow rabbit. It was a platitude at best, but an accurate one.

But Synol was drop-dead gorgeous. She looked so like Talia Oblique that Ynya yearned to call her Mama. Luckily, she caught herself.

"Synol–" she paused, a dozen replies swimming around in her head, but one stood out among the rest. Given the situation it seemed like the only prescient thing to say.

"I love you."

"I love you, too."

They hugged, for the dozenth time since they had reunited.

There was no point in arguing. Each sister looked out for the other in the only way she knew how, and quibbling over slight differences in methodology was a waste of time when the real pressure on them was to find their sisters.

Synol broke off their hug and clapped Ynya on the shoulders much harder than she normally would. "Shall we go torture this guy for information?"

Ynya smiled. "Actually, Synol, I learned something from you. Apparently if you ask the soldiers politely after you have saved their lives from a fiery demise, they will happily tell you where their bosses are keeping your sibling. We're only a few days' hike from Reyoarfjell."

"Oh good," Synol picked up a small branch from the ground, half covered in snow. "That will make my job a little easier." She palmed the branch for a moment, seemingly weighing it in her hand before breaking it.

In the distance, the captain's hoarse profanities cut off with a sickening *crunch*.

Chapter Four

I t took over five days to arrive.

After nearly a three-day journey south and east of Lyraville, they ran into their first of many patrols. New soldiers, of a variety they'd never seen before, policed the area. They wore icy-blue dyed leather uniforms, giving them a unique, but vicious, look. Unlike the hodge-podge men they'd dealt with before, all of these soldiers looked merciless and well-trained. Every one of them walked with a surety and confidence that showed they did this job on a regular basis. A few of them were accompanied by large dogs on leashes.

The sisters spent a day dodging patrols, but once they got close enough, they saw the compound.

Reyoarfjell nestled in a large valley. Along all sides, the hilltops contained guard towers, each spaced a quarter-mile apart.

Dozens of soldiers wove in between the towers, each one with a dog that snarled and barked every time they came near another patrol. None of the soldiers stopped to chat. They looked to be taking their job quite seriously.

"We need to get a better look at this place. I can't see what is over the hill and there is no way we're getting past those towers unseen," Synol said, pointing to a rise to the south. "I think we should head up there. We should be able to see over the hill from that shelf."

Ynya agreed. They backed away and spent another day making their way around to the south side of the compound.

When they finally climbed up the mountain and came out on the ledge spotted from the ground, the sisters stood in rapt amazement at the sight before them.

Reyoarfjell was huge.

The towers they'd seen from the ground were only the beginning.

Surrounding the entire compound were four massive mounds of dirt, almost a mile on each side. Atop the hill, and still stationed every quarter mile, were more of the same turrets.

"An entire mile-square prison? How many people are they housing?" Ynya's mind spun out as she tried to process just how huge the place was.

At least they knew they were heading in the correct direction.

Synol frowned. "Those towers are going to spot us for sure."

Ynya had come to the same conclusion. "It's like they knew that we were coming."

Synol shook her head. "It might look like that, but see the three towers? Each of them has two soldiers in the top, and look closely. None of them face outward. That's what the roaming pairs with dogs are for, preventing anyone traveling the country from accidentally stumbling across this place."

Synol shivered, despite the large coat she wore. "The three

towers are to keep the prisoners in, not out. Getting in will be the easy part."

"I don't plan on being in there very long. We just need to find the girls and get out."

Synol shook her head. "It took us an entire day to come in from the south side, Reyoarfjell is just too massive. Getting in, assuming we don't get killed, is going to be daunting, but finding them and escaping with our lives is going to be even harder."

Ynya felt the heated rage under her skin flare. "Are you saying we don't go in there?"

Synol flashed her own stony expression of anger. "I never said that. Don't put words in my mouth. I said it's going to be difficult, I didn't mean we don't try." She clenched her fist and leaned forward. "Just like you told me that there was no way you set fire to Marsfjord, I can't have you question my resolve. I want to see them just as much as you."

Ynya's blood chilled as she remembered that just a couple weeks prior, she'd been accused of brutally murdering her parents and burning down their entire fishing village, killing everyone inside of it.

At the time, nothing had been more important than making sure Synol understood that she was not the monster she was accused of being. Others were, but not her.

A similar guilt nudged at her voice right now. "I'm sorry. I didn't mean–"

"The issue is passed. What is the plan?"

"Plan?" Ynya was surprised Synol didn't want to talk longer about their last little spat, but she was glad that she wanted to get right back to the mission. "I think the best method to get close is to get rid of some of the roaming packs and get as much information as we can."

They spent an entire day up in the hills, observing and watching. During the day, the place swarmed with soldiers, and hundreds of prisoners milled about in a large pen in the center.

Tall timber and stone walls, completely covered in ice, prevented the mass of people inside from escaping. Beyond the walls was a zone of razor-sharp ice and rock. It was like a frost mage and an earth mage broke things into the most jagged pieces possible and embedded the remaining detritus into the earth. Shards as big as a person were visible from this distance.

Ynya suspected there was more they couldn't see.

No one was making it across that strip of land.

Each tower had two soldiers at all times. Roaming below were packs of two to three soldiers with large dogs on leashes.

Then there were the bells. Every hour the bells rang. When guard shifts occurred, the bells rang. Dinnertime, breakfast, inspection; the bells rang.

Ynya was starting to get annoyed when Synol spoke up. "I like the bells."

"You would."

Synol frowned. "There is nothing wrong with being organized. Besides, it also means that the soldiers and everyone in there are so well-trained that they might not even think about it if the bells go off at the wrong time. If we can get to those bells, we might be able to manipulate their schedule and perform shift changes closer together, thus granting our exit."

"And what about our entrance?"

"I think our best method is going to be intrusion as guards," Synol finally said.

"Only one problem with that."

"What's that?"

"Our hair. If we show up with our bright red hair like this,

I think they're all going to know who we are and why we're here."

Synol grinned. "It's a good thing all the guard uniforms have hoods to protect from the cold. Unless you want to cut yours all off, let's get in there first and worry about things later."

"Look at you, going in without a plan. Am I finally rubbing off on you?"

Synol punched her in the arm. "It's worked so far. Let's get to it."

Chapter Five

"The next patrol should be coming around the corner soon."

"Does this one have a dog?" Synol asked.

Ynya shook her head. "No, that's at least something we don't have to deal with, but we're still going to have to figure out a way to take them out without alarming anyone else."

Synol pursed her lips to a line. "Other than helping plants grow and moving stone around, I can actually change the makeup of rock." She pounded her fist into her open palm, signifying a stone. "I can change the stone to sand just as easily as I can do the reverse. I'd like to try something."

"Okay, well, they'll be here in about a minute, I saw them just duck around the corner back there."

Synol nodded, got on her knees, and leaned out over the cliff. She crouched low to the rock and began to cast.

Ynya marveled every time she felt the surge in energy around Synol. It was something else, a restrained power, like being in her father's strong arms when she was a little girl. While he had never had magic himself, his strong arms were the closest thing she could equate to what she felt emanate from Synol.

Synol kept casting, and Ynya pulled herself back from the edge. A regular pair of soldiers would be coming around the bend in the rock any second and she didn't want to risk being seen. It was bad enough that Synol had to stick her head out over the cliff to perform the spell correctly.

The clomp of boots on the hard-packed stony ground gave away the location of the two men. Their rhythmic steps revealed the well-practiced routine of a soldier.

There was a gasp from one of them, and a gurgling sound from the other.

Then silence.

Synol leaned back from the edge. Her face was bright red, like she'd just finished running or climbing up something. She huffed and her bloodshot eyes looked around with a frantic excitement.

"You alright?" Ynya knelt down.

Synol nodded, her chest heaving with large gulping swallows of air. "Yeah, just, that was a lot of work."

"Is it done?" Ynya looked between the cliff edge and her sister, not quite sure which she should tend to.

"Yeah, go check."

Ynya did, and was surprised to see...nothing. Just a path along the base of the cliff.

But then she noticed a strange swirl in the ground, and a slight movement like wind whipping around sand.

Wait, sand?

That's what was wrong, instead of hard stony ground, there was a patch of sand directly beneath them. The surface of the sand moved slightly for a few more seconds, then stopped.

Ynya noticed a small black patch and further inspection revealed that it was hair.

"You put them into quicksand?" Ynya turned to her sister. "That's kind of mean, don't you think?"

Synol shrugged, a big grin on her face. "What would you have done, overheated their heads until their brains melted? Either way, these two needed to die, and I just thought that it would be easier to get dirt off the uniform then blood. They still moving?"

Ynya looked back over the cliff. "No, but how do we get them out?"

Synol stood, her legs a bit shaky. "We'll need to head down and pull them out, but I can use the rock to help do that. Then we'll bury the bodies once more."

AFTER DISPOSING OF THE BODIES AND MODIFYING THE pant lengths slightly to ensure they fit the uniforms better, the sisters marched toward the compound.

"Are you sure this is going to work?" It was the fourth time Synol had asked the question since the bells signified a shift change.

"Will you stop asking me that? This is normal shift change, we all come in, and the others go out. If it's anything like the camp I snuck into a couple weeks ago, they might ask us for reports. Just grunt and say nothing. With as many people as they have crawling over this place, I doubt the guards will care that much."

They fell in line with other soldiers. Half a dozen dog patrols waited at the rear, probably to march in together.

As they passed by the large towers, Ynya couldn't help but

look up at the massive structures. Each one was twice as tall as Synol's old house, with thick stone bases and timbers poking out of the plaster-smoothed sides for support. She still had a hard time believing that buildings could be this tall.

They crossed through a path barely wide enough for one through the massive chunk of jagged land that surrounded Reyoarfjell. It was scary enough to see these razor-sharp hunks of stone and ice from a distance, but up-close was even worse. Bits of uniforms caught in the thousands of barbs showing that even the soldiers had to be careful.

This whole place was unforgiving, and they were willingly walking into it with no plan on how they were going to even find their sisters, let alone help them escape.

Chapter Six

Approaching the gate was surprisingly easy. No one stopped them. No one asked for a report. No one bothered looking at them closely enough to realize they didn't belong. They all just filed behind the soldiers before them.

Ynya and Synol were deathly silent, as were the rest of the soldiers. This group didn't seem to be nearly as chatty as the previous soldiers Ynya had met.

She watched the pair of soldiers in front of them. They stood at an easy attention, but one of them kept fidgeting with his hand.

He must really need to get to the bathroom.

A man carrying a bunch of papers was lowered in a basket down a pulley system. Once he reached the bottom, he shuffled his pages and walked down the ranks checking things off on the sheets, mumbling various names to himself as he did so. Once he got to the end he shouted back to the soldiers at the top of the gate. "All accounted for!"

The wall soldier yelled. "You may enter!"

A grinding noise started up behind the huge wall, then a

massive stone door melted away from the endless expanse and the line started up again.

The sisters followed the dozens of other soldiers two by two.

Ynya's skin crawled with each step. She hated having to come here, hated being here. She hated that all of this had come to her family because of the Frost Queen, and here they were infiltrating the scariest town in the realm to try to find their little sisters.

Every step reminded her just how daunting of a task it was going to be. Reyoarfjell was huge, and there was no way they could just ask around for their sisters without raising suspicion.

Once they made it past the huge wall, there was a blank patch of ground, then another wall. The outer and inner walls must have been a dozen yards from each other, providing a stark nothingness between them. A sign placed prominently on the wall warned them not to deviate from the path or risk losing limbs.

Ynya swallowed. *What have they done to the rest of the path?*

Guards roamed along the tops of both walls, watching the groups of soldiers enter in.

After going through the flat ground part, they entered another massive doorway and the view was unobstructed from here on in.

We're finally inside. We made it!

Despite making it past the walls, Ynya's heart refused to stop pounding in her chest. She couldn't decide if that was too easy, or just hard enough. Either way, she was inside the Frost Queen's internment camp for all the mages in the land.

No one wanted to come here.

But here they were.

Ynya and Synol were either very brave, or very stupid, and Ynya currently leaned toward the latter.

As the dozens of soldiers entered, they split off and began chatting. The moment they entered Reyoarfjell, the tense nature of the soldiers changed.

But it didn't change for Ynya. She was here on a mission and her stress was only beginning.

She finally got to look at the place up close for the first time.

They'd seen it from the rocky outcropping, but since the inner walls were so massive, they had really only been able to see rooftops and a bit of the pen where the prisoners spent most of their day.

Inside, it was like an entire bustling city half a mile square in each direction.

Dirt paths laid out most of the area in a structured and orderly manner. Most buildings lined the outside, leaving the center open.

The large square reminded Ynya of the town market in Holmslatr.

Around the perimeter were dozens and dozens of structures larger than Synol's old house, but none of them had any charm that a home would have. They were all just massive stone buildings with wooden roofs.

This was a place built for an army, not family. It was built for efficiency, nothing more.

Each side of the compound had differently-painted buildings. The south side they entered from was white, and going clockwise around the compound was yellow to the west, brown to the north, and finally, red to the east.

Since all the soldiers milled about, clapping each other on

their shoulders and heading off in various directions, no one seemed to be paying attention to the two newcomers.

Synol grabbed Ynya's arm to pull her off to the side. She pointed to the massive fenced-off area in the center. "Prisoners."

Ynya had noticed there were people just past the fence, but the sheer scale of the place overwhelmed her. Now that she had gotten past the towering buildings and rigid construction, she started to notice the details.

Hundreds of people milled about the large open square. All ages, genders, and varying states of dress. They were all terrifyingly thin, and most of them huddled together for warmth.

This inland Skoro district wasn't nearly as cold as the western Hyndalskyr district where Ynya hailed from. Still, the whole area got pretty cold at night and maintained a cool edge in the shade, even now in summertime.

Ynya shuddered. *How do the prisoners manage to survive the harsh winters if they aren't given clothing to keep themselves warm?*

Synol sniffed, and Ynya grabbed her hand to give a reassuring squeeze. "We need to find Finny and Meki."

Synol nodded, blinking back tears. "I know, I just wasn't expecting this. This...this is horrible."

Ynya nodded. "Yes, but we can't sit on the side and cry about it, we need to act like soldiers and go somewhere."

In the distance, from one of the south-side white buildings, a door clanged open and two soldiers exited carrying a man's naked body. He was covered in blood and appeared lifeless.

All the idle chit-chat among the soldiers ceased as everyone turned to the man.

Ynya shivered. "Let's find them and get them safe."

Chapter Seven

S ince the bloodied man had been taken toward the west, they decided to go the opposite direction. Despite how large the structure had looked from the outside, all the towers, multiple walls, and sharpened rocks had reduced the size of the inner compound by about half. The road around the huge milling area in the center appeared to be about a quarter-mile square.

It was just small enough to comfortably see from one side to the other when you stood in the center, but large enough that it still seemed incredibly massive.

As they walked down the road, nodding to soldiers who eyed them, Ynya tried to decipher all the various signs on the buildings.

"First Enlightenment? What does that mean?"

Synol shrugged. "I've been trying to figure that out for myself, too. You see that building over there?"

She pointed, and Ynya could just read the sign. "Prisoner Processing. If anyone would know where Finny or Meki or, it would be them."

Synol nodded. "I just hope we're not too late. It's been weeks since they were taken."

Ynya looked back through the massive yard in the center, at the huddled prisoners inside. "At least it's only been weeks. It could have been months or even years. How long has Reyoarfjell been around? I only ever remember Mama and Papa talk about it once when I was younger. That must have been six years ago."

Synol breathed out. "It's been open for longer than that." She stopped and turned toward Ynya. "I just realized something."

"What?"

Synol's already pale face seemed to drain of even more color.

This, in turn, raised the alarm levels of Ynya. "What is it?"

"I think Mama has been here."

The statement bored into Ynya's head, and heat rose inside her as a rush of emotion rocked her so much that she had to take a step back. "She...what?"

"I remember her talking to Papa about the Enlightenments. At the time, I never knew what they were talking about, I only knew it was related to Reyoarfjell. But I'd never heard that word uttered anywhere else until now."

Synol pointed at another sign.

Ynya's blood froze. "Third Enlightenment Processing?"

Synol visibly shivered and grabbed her arms with her hands. "Come on, I don't want to be here any longer than we need."

They came upon a building labeled Hall of Records. A half-dozen windows adorned the front, covered with shutters. In front of each shuttered window was a bench and a small table.

One guard stood by the doorway.

Ynya didn't know if soldiers needed to explain their reasons for entering buildings, but decided that marching up and making it look like she knew what she was doing would be the better choice.

She walked up to the guard, nodded perfunctorily, then grabbed the door handle and opened. Synol followed her lead.

He nodded at them, then looked back into the distance.

I can't believe that worked!

It was much warmer inside than outside. Ynya had to take down her hood lest she overheat. Synol followed suit.

The first room was empty. The entire interior looked to be carved from one piece of stone, but Ynya figured it was just built this way using earth mages' abilities. She took in the timber ceiling that was so tall she wouldn't be able to touch it even if she jumped from Synol's shoulders. A heavy wooden door adorned each wall.

"Left, right, or center?"

Ynya shrugged. "I think the center would be more likely?"

Synol nodded. "Works for me. We might need to use our magic in there, so be ready." Synol knocked on the door.

A loud cursing sound came from the other side. A woman opened the door. "What do you want?"

Synol pursed her lips. "Hello, we're looking for information on a couple prisoners that were processed here a couple weeks ago."

The woman, whose short brown hair looked like it hadn't been washed in weeks, sighed. "Do you have their ordinals?"

Synol looked at Ynya, who shrugged. "Ordinals?"

The woman's eyes opened slightly and her nostrils flared.

Inside Ynya's chest, panic rose. *Something's wrong. Why would she be asking for ordinals rather than names?*

The woman pursed her lips. Her eyebrows furrowed as she studied each of their faces. "I need to log your ordinals too, please provide them." Her eyes flicked to Ynya's right arm as she said 'ordinal.'

A memory of silvery tattoos on the two previous Skarmyord percolated in Ynya's mind. She realized the woman had silver tattoos on her right forearm as well.

Ynya jumped forward. She grabbed the woman's head and poured heat through her hands.

The woman released a scream, but it quickly faded as the heat overwhelmed her. She crumpled to the floor and Ynya grabbed her and pulled her into the room.

"Why'd you do that?"

"*Ordinals.* Did you have any idea what that meant?"

"No, but I was going to ask her to explain."

"You think she would have explained something to us that we should have known already? Did you notice her eyes? She knew we weren't who we said we were."

Synol's eyes went wide. "What does that mean?"

"It means we should hurry."

The records room turned out to be a lot smaller than they expected. A large wooden desk stood in the center, with a dozen cabinets along the back and side walls. Each one contained three drawers with metal pulls.

On the front of each cabinet drawer was a small placard with words on them.

Ynya scanned the room.

"These four have First, Second, Third, and Fourth Enlightenments."

Synol replied. "Here is one for Discarded. Should we look here first?"

Ynya shuddered, but shook her head. "Let's follow the

path they normally would have. Is there one for new prisoners or something?"

"Here." Synol pointed at the draw in the corner. "Arrivals."

"That should work."

Opening the first drawer, they found it contained a number of ledgers. Each one had date ranges stamped into the outside leather. The one in the front was for the last two months.

"There."

Synol grabbed it out and took it to the desk. Ynya began to close the drawer, then stopped. She scanned over the ledgers.

"These go back years."

Ynya's chest tightened.

She opened up the drawer underneath it. "These go back even further. This is before I was born."

Panic rose higher in her tight chest.

She moved to the final drawer in the stack, and stopped. "These are much, much older, Synol." Her heart pounded as she scanned the dates.

"How far?"

Ynya held back a shiver while the hairs stood on her arm.

"They go back a hundred years."

Chapter Eight

❦

S ynol opened the ledger. "We need to find the girls."
Ynya nodded, closing the drawer. "Yes."

But her mind couldn't stop thinking about what was in that drawer. *How has this prison been going on for so long, yet I've only heard about it recently? Is it something the Frost Queen started, or is this something that has been going on longer than her reign?*

The notion of those hundreds of ledgers terrified her. She turned and looked through the room with a newfound horror. *Each of these cabinets list thousands of names over at least a hundred years. How many people have come through here?*

"Ynya, I found them!"

That snapped her back to reality. "You what?"

Ynya stepped over to Synol, who had her finger planted on two rows about midway through the ledger. Each page listed four rows, for four people.

"Age twelve, gender female, hair red. Name Finny Oblique. This is her. She and Meki. They were processed three weeks ago. There are a few numbers here, but I'm not sure what they mean."

Synol pointed to the column headers.

"E-one?"

"Enlightenment?"

"Maybe, but how do we tell where they were taken?"

The door burst open with a loud *crack*.

In a blur, half a dozen soldiers clad in blue attire flooded through the door and surrounding both girls.

Ynya flared her heat, routing it to her hands. Before she could do anything with it, a flash of silver filled her vision and she was stabbed three times. Thigh, middle, shoulder.

Each time the blade pierced her skin, she relived memories from long ago. Even though she knew the attack only took a half second, it seemed like an age. Ynya watched each blade strike true, and with each hit she wished she knew how to defend against their attacks.

She thought back to the lesson she had learned from Miss-Miss. *You only get one chance to attack them, because after that, they own you.*

That was the only way Ynya had managed to take out the woman in white. Even then, it was an incredibly close battle, and one she had only won because the woman was hobbled and overextended for the final strike.

Ynya crumpled to the ground in a heap as she felt her magic dissipate into a mist of nothingness.

Beside her, Synol did the same. Her head hit the table with a *thump* as she fell forward. She lay motionless across the ledger.

"So, who do we have here?"

A man clad all in red leather strolled through the doorway. He was tall and muscular, with a broad chest and a short well-trimmed beard. His hair was shaved off, leaving his head shiny in the lantern light.

He wove his fingers together and cracked his knuckles.

"Sorry we weren't here to see you all personally, but we had already flagged you as suspicious when you entered the compound. Not knowing the proper hand signals made you stand out."

Hand signals?

"But I am curious to meet someone with the audacity to infiltrate a place such as this. Normally everyone wants to escape, so why would anyone want to come in? I told my soldiers to let you in and we kept our distance to watch where you went."

He stepped closer and loomed over Ynya. His bright red outfit and pale skin made him almost look like he was on fire.

"So how about we see what all the fuss is about, shall we?"

He grabbed Synol by the arm and yanked her from the desk. She crumpled to the floor.

Two soldiers who had been standing over the sisters with silver daggers sheathed them and stepped out of the way.

He looked up at the other soldiers in the room. "You can go, we have this. We'll need to send them for processing, though, so notify the Inscriber that we have two unscheduled entries."

"Of course, Sir."

All but two of the soldiers left, leaving the door open.

The man in red picked up the ledger and looked it over. "Oh. Oh my, you ladies must be the two I've been hearing so much about. The Oblique sisters, I assume?"

He folded up the ledger and handed it to one of the soldiers, then squatted down to get closer. "Let's get a better look at you both."

The other soldier grabbed Synol and wrenched her to a sitting position. The first soldier set the ledger down and did the same to Ynya.

They weren't gentle.

The soldiers forced Ynya into the row of cabinets behind her, cracking her head on the dense wood. The pain was intense and made her feel nauseous as heat bloomed through her head and into her torso.

The man in red grabbed Synol's chin, moving her side to side and looking at her face. "You must be Synol, the older one. I thought you were coming here in a carriage. You should have just stuck with the plan, because you are now going to experience things the hard way."

He pulled his hand away and grabbed Ynya's chin.

Revulsion replaced the pain in an instant, as soon as he touched her. She wanted to bite, but she couldn't move.

"And you must be the fire one I've heard so much about. You have caused a lot of grief for the soldiers in Hyndalskyr district, I have to say. Many of the soldiers here have friends who died by your hand, so enjoy how they treat you for that."

He stood. "Shackle them first, then take them to the yard and into processing."

"Yes, Sir."

One of the soldiers reached into a pouch and pulled out a strange-looking apparatus with a handle and a clamp on one side. The handle had some kind of a trigger mechanism.

She put the object to Synol's ear, and pulled the trigger.

Synol grunted.

When the soldier pulled the apparatus away, Synol's ear bled. A small silver earring was locked in her ear.

The soldier loaded another round into the ear piercer and punctured Ynya's ear, too.

Her connection to magic disappeared.

It was like being stabbed with the silver daggers, but worse. With the daggers, the magic was still present, but too far away to be felt or touched. This one removed the magic entirely.

Ynya felt empty inside as the heat she'd enjoyed her entire life disappeared. The cold right next to her heart, the one she'd received from her mother and still hadn't figured out how to activate, disappeared as well.

Gone.

She remembered how foreign her mother's magic felt to her when she first received it. But now that it was gone, too, she realized just how much she had come to enjoy the constant reminder of her mother's presence right beside her heart. Even though she hadn't figured out how to use it yet, it had been with her long enough that it was now a part of her. It no longer felt foreign to her.

Ynya liked carrying that piece of her mother with her.

Now it was gone, along with all her abilities.

She tried desperately to pull the earrings out, but it was no use. Stronger magic than hers held them in place.

The ever-present rage flared but quickly subsided, her magic unable to fuel it any longer.

"Oh, and in case you were wondering where your sisters were," the man in red spoke from the doorway, "one is currently being processed here, but another was removed from the program almost immediately. Seems she didn't have what it takes for her Majesty's Army, so we disposed of her."

Chapter Nine

Prisoner 1267062201 watched from the chair as a man came into the lab.

She had been strapped to this chair for the last three hours, and instructed to wait.

She had complied.

She always complied.

It was how things were done here at the compound. You complied, or there were consequences.

But the voice continued to tell her not to comply. The small voice she constantly pushed away told her to stand up. It told her to break the shackles around her wrists and ankles and leave this place. It told her to find her sisters, and her Mama.

She told the voice no. She was going to follow instructions this time.

It was the least painful way.

"2201, I see you are awake."

The man approached. He wore brown leather clothes and a long apron that might have been white at some point. His boots were finely stitched and covered in dark red stains.

Everything he wore was covered in dark red stains.

He carried a number of books and papers and placed those on the desk in the corner of the room.

After shuffling around for a bit, he pulled a stool from behind the desk and placed it in front of her.

He sat down, groaning with each movement.

"I am the Translator, at least that's what everyone calls me around here. You have been expedited, and I am most excited to try some things on you."

He grabbed her right wrist and turned it, to read the ordinals etched on her inner arm. As he read, his eyes widened. "Oh my, you have quite the number of amazing gifts, and those have already been enhanced. I say, we are going to have so much fun."

He pulled back her sleeve. "Gods Above."

He pulled back the top of her shirt to expose her shoulder, where the fresh numbers had just been etched the day before. The skin around them was still raw and painful.

The voice told her to bite him, but she pushed it away.

"And Gods Below. All the way to the middle of your chest. We don't have many of you, unfortunately. We have to make do with what we have, and who we can round up. But every so often a fine specimen such as yourself comes into my office and I get to fine-tune my methods."

He released her shirt and stood.

The man in the apron turned a wooden crank on the side of her chair.

Her chair elongated and flattened, straightening her from a sitting position to standing. With a *creak*, the board fell back and latched into something.

Now she lay on a table.

She'd been on a lot of tables in the recent past. She spent most of her time on tables, being Enlightened.

He grabbed her right wrist and turned her hand, slapping the inside of her elbow. "Of all the places you've been, I have to tell you that this one is the most exciting. The treatment that I deliver here is unlike any that you have experienced in the other centers. This one is the pinnacle of our modern science engineering. The best of the best!"

He cackled, which devolved into a cough. "The point is, this is the end goal. This is why we are here. This is why I've been here for so long, extending my life one generation at a time in order to complete my work for Her Majesty. This is my place, and she had all this built just for me. Many have come through here over the years, sadly not many have survived, but each time I get closer and closer."

He sighed, looking across the room with a distance in his eyes. "And yet some that should have come here didn't." He clucked his tongue.

A smaller table stood beside the one 2201 lay on. It held several vials full of different-colored liquids, glass tubes with glass rods inside them, and needles.

Big ones.

The man grabbed a needle and twisted it into the end of one of the narrow glass tubes with a rod inserted into the other end. He dipped the needle's point into a vial filled with light green liquid and pulled the glass rod out of the tube just a little. The green liquid filled in the air gap left by the rod. He pointed the needle up and pushed on the rod until the liquid squirted out the top, then stopped.

He repeated the activity four more times, each time pulling a different-colored liquid in the glass tube.

Finally, he placed his hand on her right shoulder. "This,

like all changes, is going to hurt, but you've already been taught to endure pain." He paused, then read the ordinals etched on her shoulder once again. His eyes flared.

"Quite a lot of pain it seems."

He cleared his throat. "I do have to say, as a scientist, I pride myself on facts and experiments. I like looking at data as empirically as possible, but there is something about you that I get a little giddy about, seeing just how much potential you have locked up inside your little red-haired body."

He grinned, showing off his crooked, yellowed teeth. "I know I shouldn't be excited about this since so many of my experiments fail catastrophically, but the good news is that I think I have all the kinks worked out this time. My last patient is still alive and that bodes very well for you."

He paused to jot something down on the paper.

The voice told her to break out of the shackles and stick the needle in his neck. She told the voice to go away. She was doing her duty. She was being obedient.

He grabbed up the syringe and plunged it into her arm. "Let's see how this works, shall we?"

As the green liquid disappeared into her arm, the voice inside her head screamed.

Unadulterated fire spread from her arm through her entire body. She shook in the restraints.

The voice grew louder as the fire burned through her. With every passing second, it grew more and more prescient as the pain continued to build.

She couldn't take it anymore, and she listened. She turned her head and listened to the voice.

The voice told her to blow.

She obeyed.

Prisoner 1267062201 sucked in a massive amount of air, and blew it out in one massive gale.

All around her, the torrent of magic surged throughout the small room, buoyed by her pain and anguish. Every experiment she'd gone through in the last few weeks bubbled to the surface and for the slightest second she remembered a name.

Ynya.

Ynya would save her.

The voice inside her took over completely and whipped wind around inside the room, trying to destroy it. The wind howled in her ears, and the man screamed beside her, holding on to a leather strap attached to the chair.

Something pierced her shoulder and she lost all magic.

All was still, and the voice receded, happy that she had listened once again.

Chapter Ten

"Let me go you Gods-Sided Assholes! I will kill every one your mothers, and all of your family!"

Ynya fought back as much as she could the second she got control of her mouth.

But without her magic, she was just a waif-thin girl in the north.

She shivered now that her heat didn't work. The soldiers had removed the stolen uniforms and Ynya only had her thin red dress.

Synol bore the indignity of being hauled around in silence.

Ynya wasn't quite sure what to make of it. *Doesn't Synol want to escape? Doesn't she want to rail against her captors? Why isn't she at least trying to get out of her bonds, or at very least kick the soldiers in the mouth to give them a broken tooth or jaw or something?*

Synol had a frame much more designed for athletics than Ynya. One kick from her would leave an indelible impression on the guard.

One of the solders grabbed a baton and slammed it down

on the back of Ynya's neck for the third time since they'd left the records building. She didn't even care anymore. It hurt, but her anger kept her focused and alert.

"Quiet! We have to get you Ordained and you don't have to be conscious for the process."

Ordained?

Ynya glanced sideways to Synol, who didn't return her look. Her head was down and her eyes focused as the guards led her through the street.

They stopped outside another large building–they all seemed to look the same other than the colors and the sign out front.

Ynya hated it. Everything was the same. There was no flow to the place. It was too organized, structured. None of the buildings had any life.

Nor did the inhabitants.

All of them wore a glazed-over expression, like they were going through the motions.

Well, I'll be the one to give them emotion.

Ynya struggled again against her bonds. But the soldier simply dropped her into a chair and before she knew it, five large shackles bolted around her.

An old woman came out of the door from the main building. "What do we have here? It's not processing day."

"Direct from the Warden. He wants these two Ordained immediately and moved into testing."

The old woman, who had long silver hair done up in a bun behind her head, hobbled over to Synol and grabbed her by her chin. She examined Synol for a moment, mumbling to herself about facial features, then turned to Ynya.

She smiled. If they'd been in different situations, Ynya might have liked this woman. She seemed kindly enough, but she had that soulless look in her eyes like all the other soldiers.

"Oh you are a feisty one, aren't you?"

Ynya shook her diminutive frame in the massive wood chair and shackles. "Come here and find out, you old bag."

The woman's bushy eyebrows rose at the insult. "You have quite the mouth on you, young woman. But I treat everyone the same here. As long as you don't hurt me, I'll do my best to not hurt you. But I have a job to do, so I best get on with it."

She turned to her building but stopped after a couple steps. "I suppose we are going to spend a little bit of time together, I should introduce myself. I'm the Inscriber. You both look very familiar. You don't happen to have two younger sisters, do you?"

Ynya gritted her teeth.

The old woman smirked, then stepped through the door.

Ynya raged. She snapped at anything that was close, shook her shackles, and screamed. She didn't even know what came out of her mouth, but she tried to get as imaginative as she could with her epithets.

One of the soldiers backhanded her in the jaw. "Quiet."

Finally, Synol spoke. "Ynya."

"What?" Ynya was pissed. She was mad at herself for getting caught, mad at Synol for not being as angry as she.

"Save your energy. There are times to fight and times to wait."

Ynya wanted to explode at her sister, but the words from Miss-Miss echoed in her ears. *Smoke, not fire.*

Instead of replying, Ynya simply went limp.

Fine, if they're going to be like this, I'll play their game.

The Inscriber came back, carrying a small box.

She opened the box on the table and removed a number of

components; bowls, bottles of silvery and clear ink, and cloths. Then, she took out a couple of needles that reminded Ynya of the ones her Mama used to make dresses that were always too big for her waifish daughter. Only these needles were bigger. Much bigger.

The old woman turned to face Synol.

"I have to Ordain you, you understand that?"

Without turning to the old woman, Synol nodded. "Do what you have to do, and I'll do likewise."

The Inscriber turned to Ynya. "See? I like your sister. She's a smart one."

The woman picked up the small vial with clear liquid in it and soaked the rag in the solution.

"This is just a bit of antiseptic, to keep you from becoming infected. It doesn't hurt."

She dabbed it on Synol's inner right arm.

Whatever antiseptic was, it didn't seem to phase Synol one bit.

She then poured a bit of the silver liquid into a shallow bowl, and grabbed a large needle. "This...not so much."

Beside her, one of the guards shifted. Ynya couldn't be sure, but it seemed they had a visceral reaction to what was about to take place.

The Inscriber dipped the needle into the bowl, coming away with just the slightest amount of silver liquid clinging to the tip. She poked it into Synol's arm. It must not have hurt too much because Synol winced once after the first needle poke, but then continued to wear a serious and emotionless expression thereafter.

The Inscriber worked for nearly an hour, dipping and poking over and over, hundreds, possibly thousands of times. Every minute, she would wipe the area with one of the rags. It came back with a mixture of red blood and whatever the silvery liquid was. She went through nearly a dozen rags, eventually leaving a significant pile on the ground.

Finally, the Inscriber sat up. "Perfect."

She turned to Ynya.

Ynya had tried to see what design the woman was doing, but couldn't see past her back.

"Your turn. But I need to take a short rest. My back isn't what it used to be. I'll be right back."

She left through her door.

"Did that hurt?"

Synol didn't reply.

"What did she put on your arm?"

Again, Synol didn't reply.

Behind them, the chimes rang out, signifying some kind of shift change.

Ynya wanted to scream. The desire to yell boiled just under the surface, but the constantly throbbing from the repeated blows to her head reminded her to keep her anger in check. The notion of her little sister being discarded tried to work into her head, but she pushed out the thought. *Now is not the time to dwell on what the Warden said.*

The door opened as the Inscriber returned.

"Alright, young woman, time for yours."

She reorganized the silvery liquid closer, and pulled out the clear liquid. "Antiseptic again."

The antiseptic smelled of harsh liquor. But it was cold to Ynya's skin when it went on.

The Inscriber dipped the ink into the well once again, and looked at Ynya. "You ready?"

Ynya huffed. "I don't care."

The old woman smiled. "Oh, I think you care a lot, but none of that matters now."

She poked into Ynya's skin and a dense hot pain shot through Ynya's arm. Far more than just a localized needle poke, it was a raging torrent of hot and cold, a mixture she'd never experienced before.

It was pure untainted pain. Ynya whimpered, trying to swallow back a scream. Tears poured from her eyes at the realization of how much that hurt. Just one needle prick and her entire arm throbbed. She'd rather be stabbed a hundred times from those silver daggers than by this needle.

The old woman stopped. "Now, now. Your sister was silent."

Tears streamed down Ynya's cheek and she looked up to her sister. Synol met her gaze, a morose expression on her face, and a single tear matching Ynya's.

Synol mouthed, "I love you."

The Inscriber punched the needle into Ynya's arm again and again. Every single time, the intense pain tore through her body.

After the tenth prick, Ynya couldn't hold back and cries of anguish replaced the whimpers.

After twenty, Ynya sobbed.

After the hundredth, Ynya bawled.

She bawled for her mother, she bawled for her father. She pleaded to be given a rest because the pain was so intense.

The entire time, Synol's gaze never left Ynya.

Chapter Eleven

Ynya didn't think it would end, but eventually, the pain stopped. A dozen bloodied rags were piled on the floor when the woman stood. "All yours."

She started for her door, then turned. "For what it's worth," she pulled the sleeve back on her own arm, exposing her entire forearm. Silver numbers were etched on her arm, then she pulled down her shirt from her shoulder to show more numbers on her upper inner arm. "Everyone here has them. It's just part of life."

With that, she left.

The two soldiers walked them to the large holding pen in the center of camp. "When your number gets called, you better come find us. If we have to find you, there will be consequences."

They walked through another double fence to get into the main holding pen in the center, where Ynya had seen all the milling prisoners when they first entered into this place.

They both stood there for a minute, taking in their new locale.

The yard was massive. Most of the dirt was packed clay and rock.

At least two hundred prisoners milled about in the space. Most huddled together for warmth. Everyone was dirty, malnourished, and many wore nothing but rags.

It was incredibly easy to tell the new ones from the others that had been here a while based on how dirty their clothes were.

Ynya was suddenly aware of just how bright and frivolous her dress was at the moment. She felt sorry that everyone with the mud-stained clothes had to look at her. She didn't deserve having such nice clothes if others had to survive on less. She wanted to grab mud from a corner and coat herself in it. She didn't want to stand out in this place.

Synol removed her coat, and walked up to a small group of people huddled together. The woman had no shirt, and huddled with her daughter in her lap and two more children on other side of her.

"For you."

The woman took it without a word, but nodded appreciably to Synol.

Synol came back to stand next to Ynya. "I'm sorry she hurt you."

Ynya looked down at her arm for the first time since the woman started her inscribing process. Blocky, silver letters went from her wrist and ended halfway to her elbow, eight numbers.

"12670713022?"

"It's today's date." Synol replied, not looking at her arm. "I have 01 at the end and you have 02. It's today's date with a unique identifier on it. Everyone here has one, so you can tell what date they were logged into the camp."

She pointed at the woman who now wore Synol's coat. "She's been here for two years."

"Damn."

"The woman who tattooed us has been here for sixty one."

Ynya didn't know what to say to that.

Behind them, someone yelled. "Ynya?"

Ynya remembered the voice, but couldn't quite place where she had heard it before.

Ynya whirled around.

There stood Joanne and Tyrain, two of the mages who had helped Ynya escape from the caravan.

Joanne was a little thinner than last time she'd seen her, but still had that feisty look in her eye. Tyrain looked older somehow, despite only being twelve. His face had hardened somewhat and he had an edgy demeanor he didn't have before.

Ynya couldn't hold back her emotions anymore. All the pain she'd experienced, all the anguish in the eyes of those around her, all the loss she'd gone through bubbled to the surface. She'd never gone this long without her magic before, even though the multiple times she'd been stabbed by the Skarmyord. Part of her worried she was never going to get it back.

That part didn't want to imagine what life would be like.

And now, seeing two mages she'd help set free in the past just broke her heart.

It was too much. She couldn't keep everything bottled up anymore.

She fell on Joanne, who held her upright while Ynya cried on her shoulder.

Her right forearm burned, but she didn't care. The pain wasn't the issue anymore.

After a couple minutes, the grief melted away and turned

into a seething rage again, just below her skin. She missed the heat, but she wanted to maintain that edge.

"What are you doing here?" She finally asked, giving Tyrain a hug.

"Shortly after we escaped, we headed north, trying to get to Lyraville."

"Oh no, and that place was crawling with soldiers."

Joanne nodded. "Yeah. We took out a couple of them, stole some food, and managed to hole ourselves up to the south. We woke up one morning and Hans was gone, took everything we had. We searched for him, but couldn't find where he'd gone."

Tyrain filled in the rest of the story. "We couldn't go back to Holmslatr, so we tried to make it past Lyraville, but ended up getting caught in the middle of the night. They brought us here and that's been it for the last week or so."

Ynya frowned. "Lyraville is safe now. We managed to kill all the soldiers there and there are no more patrols between there and Holmslatr anymore. I'm sorry you got caught."

She looked between them. "So Hans left, but what about Firtze?"

"He was taken."

"Taken?"

Tyrain pointed toward the south, where the white-roofed buildings sat. "The Translator came and took him. Once you go to him, you're never seen from again."

Ynya tried to process what she'd just heard. Translator? What did that mean? She was about to ask about Finny and Meki, but Synol spoke up.

"What is this place? What are any of us doing here? We just arrived trying to sneak in and were captured. We just got these horrible tattoos and I don't even know what is going on."

Joanne lifted her right arm, a series of numbers were on it, more than what the two girls had just gotten. "Ordinals. We all get them, and they hurt like hell every-time."

"Wait, you get more?" Ynya asked.

Synol grabbed Ynya's arm gently, a signal to keep quiet. "Please, start at the beginning, I need to know what this place is and its purpose, so we can start puzzling out where our sisters were taken."

Ynya glared at her sister, but she remembered Synol's unending tear-filled gaze while she was getting her ordinals. Synol deserved to ask any question she wanted.

Joanne sighed and took a deep break before launching into her explanation.

"Reyoarfjell has been around for a long time. It's a re-education camp, or at least that's what I keep hearing them call it." She pointed to the north, at the brown buildings. "You are going to get tested first, to find out how many abilities you have, that's when you get more ordinals on your skin depending on how many abilities you have and how powerful you are."

She pointed at the additional figured on her arm that stopped just past her elbow. "Anyone with more abilities or incredibly powerful abilities is taken for further processing."

"And what about these?" Synol jiggled the earring they all wore in their ears.

"It's like the daggers used by the Skarmyord. It blocks your magic. They have to take it out when they test you, but you're going to be strapped down." She paused, her face taking on a somber look. "The testing is very painful."

Synol nodded, rubbing Joanne's arm. "I'm sorry."

Joanne nodded. "Firtze came back with numbers past his shoulder." She pointed at a spot on her upper chest, just below her clavicle. "He wasn't back here long before they took him to the Enlightenments."

"Enlightenments?" Ynya and Synol asked together. They looked at each other, sharing a stricken look between them.

Ynya spoke first. "We've heard that term before. What is it?"

"That's the re-education part of it. I personally haven't gone through any of them yet. Like many of the ones huddled here, we are tested, then just left alone. Anyone with higher abilities is taken first, so many people just live their lives here until one day you are picked for something and taken away. The only thing I do know, is that the Skarmyord, the Queen's elite guards, are trained here too. Rumor is that the better your abilities, the faster you are put to training and sent out into the field, but there is something else going on here that no one seems to talk about."

"What's that?"

She shrugged. "I don't know. I see it in everyone's eyes though. Some big secret no one talks about with anyone. Everyone knows, but no one will talk about it. Next time someone is dragged out of the white buildings bloodied and limp, I want you to watch everyone's reactions."

Synol asked, "So, have you seen anyone here that matches our description? We're here looking for our sisters. Have you seen them?"

Both Joanne and Tyrain shook their heads. "Sorry, we haven't seen anyone with red hair."

Around them, the bells chimed once again.

Ynya growled. "I hate those things."

Joanne nodded. "They are annoying, but that's nothing compared to what they put you through here. You will get used to them pretty soon. They have different melodies to tell you when it's time to wake up, go to bed, time for breaks, and food."

Joanne pointed to the large tower in the northeast corner of the pen. "That's where the chimes are. I actually know the guy who rings them."

"Rings them?"

"We all have jobs here, or at least most of us do. You'll probably be assigned to work in the kitchen or something, we basically do all the work the soldiers don't want to do, but if you're a good prisoner they give you the easier jobs. Ringing the bells is one of them. Gustav got himself a nice job there."

She pointed off to the north west corner. "I have a friend that works one of the gates, as well. He stays in the barracks with the rest of the soldiers. I'll show him once he comes out. You're going to love him. He's got this incredible skin that you don't find on anyone up this far north."

Synol sighed.

"What's wrong?" Ynya asked.

Synol frowned. "It's just that we're in here, and Finny and Meki aren't. I also can't stop thinking about what The Warden said to us."

Emotions flooded Ynya at the mention of that. She'd been trying to forget she ever met that man.

"Don't think about it."

Synol shook her head. "I can't stop thinking about it. What did he mean by that?"

Ynya grabbed Synol around the neck and touched their foreheads together. "Synol. Listen to me. Focusing on what he said isn't going to do any good for any of us. Focus on the positive. We know one of them is in here, so our mission is to find her and get her out. We can't change the past, we can only keep moving forward."

Synol nodded, pained grooves in her forehead betrayed the stress behind her bloodshot eyes. "I know. It's just that we're now in here and we not only need to find them, but we have to escape now, too."

Chapter Twelve

The next morning, Joanne took the sisters around the entire perimeter. She explained that everyone called it the Pit, even though it wasn't deeper than the rest of the complex.

The four sides to Reyoarfjell were laid out in a mostly logical manner.

Prisoners were housed to the east, while soldiers and other staff lived on the west.

The north was mostly administration and Enlightenment buildings. All the testing was performed in those buildings. It was where Ynya and Synol had found the Hall of Records and where they had received their ordinals.

The south was where the Skarmyord trained.

Ynya watched as two soldiers carried a naked woman covered in blood out of one of the white-roofed buildings. No one spoke while they dragged her body through the road. In fact, everyone, prisoners and guards alike, seemed serene, almost reverent about the whole event.

To Ynya, it was strikingly clear just how trivial their lives were when it came to the service of the Frost Queen.

If you die, there will always be another mage to test and push and train. There will always been another mage to torture until they either break, or live long enough to become a Skarmyord.

Ynya tried her hardest to ignore the constant reminder of the final words of the Warden.

Seems she didn't have what it takes for her Majesty's Army, so we disposed of her.

Ynya balled her fists as she noticed the silver tattoos on the woman. It was difficult to see through the blood, but her ordinals went from her wrist to past her shoulder.

Synol came up behind Ynya and put her hand on Ynya's shoulder. "We need a plan."

Ynya nodded, but kept her gaze as the soldiers disappeared into another building at the far edge of the complex.

"I want to burn it down. Every bit of this place."

"I know, but we can't use magic."

That familiar rage built under her skin once again. "I know that!"

Synol took a step back. "Ynya."

"No!" Ynya whirled on her sister. "Don't placate me. I want to be mad and I'm going to be mad. I have every right to be pissed off about what they are doing to me here."

Synol looked at the ground.

"No retort? No snappy comeback?"

Synol looked up at Ynya. She wore the most pointed, angry face Ynya had seen in a long time. Synol slapped Ynya across the face, then grabbed her by the throat and shoved her into the fence.

"Doing to you? Doing to *you?* Have you looked around?

It's not just *you* who is in pain, Ynya. I'm sorry that things aren't going perfectly for *you*, but we're here now and we have to deal with it. There are other people in pain here and I want to try to figure out a way to get our sisters back *and* try to help these people. They all deserve it. Look around and notice that there are more people in here than just you."

Ynya stood still, shocked mostly. The slap hurt, but Synol's righteous outburst pained her the most. Every now and again, the rage she felt came out in Synol, and every time it was such a poignant fury.

She relaxed, looking away from her sister. "I know, Synol. I do."

Synol released her and stormed off.

Joanne cleared her throat. "Sorry."

Ynya rubbed at her jaw. "It's not her fault. I can't keep my thoughts to myself and she can't open up about what's going on in her head."

Joanne smirked. "You two are a lot alike. Both fiery and angry."

Ynya nodded. "Yeah, I suppose we are. So, what do I need to know about these Enlightenments?"

Joanne pointed to the north. "I just know the first two are up there." She turned and pointed back at the building to the south, from which the soldiers had dragged the broken body. "Third happens here."

"You said that's where the Skarmyord are trained?"

She nodded. "Yeah. Though as you can see, not everyone survives the training, whatever it is."

"And no one here knows what goes on behind those doors?"

"Some do, but they don't talk about it. A lot of the people here who go through the First and Second Enlightenment come back spouting about how amazing the Frost Queen is. They talk about how she's a great leader, and how life here is better because she's guiding everything for us."

"Seriously? They like being here?"

Joanne shrugged. "I guess. I don't know how someone can come out of there with cuts and bruises all over their body and smile about how the Frost Queen is somehow taking care of them. I just don't get it."

Ynya balled her fists again. "I don't either."

"1267071301 and 1267071302!" Two guards stood at one of the entrances to the inner compound shouting numbers.

"What's his problem?"

Joanne grabbed Ynya's wrist and turned her hand over. Ynya winced at the pain that shot up her arm once again.

"Hey!"

"That's yesterday's date, isn't it?" Joanne studied the numbers on Ynya's arm. "They're calling you and Synol."

"Ynya pulled her hand back, cradling it to keep the raw newly-tattooed flesh safe. "Let them call all they want, what are they going to do, search every one of us?"

Joanne's eyes went wide. "No, but you don't want to be here if they do. Synol!" Joanne called into the crowd in the direction Synol had left. Ynya's sister came back looking eerily calm.

Joanne grabbed Synol by the hand and spun Ynya around to face the guards. "You and Ynya need to go!"

"1267071301 and 1267071302! Final warning!"

"We are here," Synol announced. "No need to get anyone in trouble. What is it?"

Ynya grumbled, but kept her mouth shut. She wasn't happy about Synol taking charge of their situation. *But I suppose now isn't the time to get pissy about it.*

One of the guards looked at a board he held in his hands. "Pre-Enlightenment testing, come on."

Synol took a step forward. "I'm coming."

Ynya didn't move.

After a second, Synol stopped and whirled on her. "Ynya, we don't have time for one of your fits. Come on."

Ynya shook her head. "I'm not throwing a fit, I'm resisting. They have me here without my permission, they captured us, and you're just going along with them?"

"Zero-two, if you do not comply I will force you to comply." The guard removed a small metal rod from his belt, and, with a throwing motion, the rod grew to about four times the length. He held it out in front of him.

"Ynya, please. We can fight another day."

Ynya smiled. "They will have to force me, because I'm not coming." She turned on the whole place, raising her voice. "You hear that everyone? I'm not going with them!"

"Ynya," Synol pleaded.

"No! Not today, Synol. Today you don't tell me what I can and cannot do. I will fight them with every breath I have. I will fight for our freedom, I will fight to get my magic back. I'll kick and scream and claw and–"

The guard touched her stomach with the pole.

An incredible surge of lighting shot through her body, starting from her stomach and ending in each extremity.

She fell to the ground. Her shout stopped mid-word as her throat closed up. nothing but a gargling sound made it out.

Every part of her hurt. Her muscles twitched uncontrollably and she could no longer control any part of herself. The last thing she remembered before she blacked out was peeing herself while hundreds of sorrowful faces looked on.

Chapter Thirteen

Ynya woke with a bucket full of frigid water splashed onto her.

She sat up spitting water from her mouth when someone threw another two buckets, one after the other.

Light shone in front of her, but she was blinded by the water in her eyes.

Water went up her nose, and she coughed and sputtered to get it out of there. She breathed in more and her lungs burned from the intrusion.

"What the hell is going on?" Ynya coughed again, wiping water from her eyes.

A man's voice responded. "Next time, obey instructions and we won't have to clean you up when you shit yourself."

A woman's voice laughed, and Ynya heard the sound of footsteps as the two guards retreated. The light went with them, but just before everything went pitch black, she saw enough to know that she was in a cell.

She reached out to judge the cell's size. It was small, just barely enough for her to sit up in with two inches overhead.

Her hands found the bars, thick and coated in a fine powder, probably rust.

"When are you going to learn, Ynya?" Synol finally spoke up in the darkness.

Ynya spat, then swore repeatedly.

Synol didn't say anything for a long time. Then finally, "I'm sorry you had to go through that."

Ynya didn't feel like talking, but she was curious. "Did I really shit myself?"

"Yes. It wasn't very ladylike."

Ynya laughed. "Fuck ladylike. I can do this all day."

Synol sighed.

Ynya did feel a little bad about how she had acted, but she'd been using her magic for so long that she didn't know how to function without it anymore. That familiar burn in her breast guided her actions and spurred her to anger when she needed it most.

Synol wouldn't understand—

Actually, that wasn't correct. Synol did understand. Just because she didn't publicly use her magic, didn't mean that she didn't have it.

Ynya still wasn't used to the idea that she wasn't the only one of her siblings to have magic. She'd always been the outgoing one, the one flaunting her ability to her siblings, and using it with a recklessness that had driven a wedge between her and her older sister.

Ynya wondered how her actions affected her mother, Talia.

Talia Oblique had magic. That was never at question, but she'd always been a restrained woman. She was the type to always put duty before personal comfort. Even up to her last breath, lying there in the frozen tundra of their burned-down home, she had put duty to her family before herself.

For a moment, Ynya reached inside herself to touch the magic that thrummed alongside her heart. Then she remembered, she didn't have the magic anymore. *The magic that my mother died to give me, after enduring atrocities and violations that no woman should ever have to endure, and for what?*

Ynya was without any of her magics now. She couldn't touch anything – her own fire, her mother's unending beat. None of it was there anymore.

Despite the lack of inner heat, anger flared once again in her breast. Not fueled by magic, but lacking none of the vitriol and fury of one wronged, she knew what she needed to do.

Before allowing herself to second guess the thought, Ynya grabbed the earring in her right ear. She fought past the strong magic keeping it there and ripped it from it's resting place.

Pain shot through her head, reaching her vocal cords and escaping from her mouth in a torrential scream.

But the scream was not just for the pain, for, just as the earring exited her body, her magic rushed back with a vengeance.

Heat flooded in her chest, filling every inch of her small frame with fervor unfettered.

The cold beat returned too, stoic and unwavering. It was almost like her mother was back in her life, standing right next to her.

And she wouldn't waste a second of it.

Synol gasped.

Ynya realized that her hair had fired to life.

Every strand of her long red hair was ablaze with vibrant white hot light. She looked at her sister, who sat in her own cage right next to hers. The brilliant light completely washed out Synol's pale face.

"I will not be contained!" Ynya screamed. It felt so good to have her magic back, and now she needed to use the newfound power.

Grabbing the bars of her cage, Ynya poured immense heat into the iron. In a few seconds, the metal was soft, able to be pulled apart. She did just that, widening the gap between them until her body fit.

A mere heartbeat later, she stood outside her cage.

Ynya looked around. More than a dozen cages filled the stone-walled room, each one set on top of a slab of rock to keep them elevated off the floor. Each cage was just large enough to contain one person, but not enough for comfort, or to stretch out in any one direction.

They were clearly designed to drive the prisoner mad. Each one was just far enough away from the other that no prisoner could touch another.

Close enough to see, but far enough away to prevent human contact.

Her blood boiled as she took in the sight.

Synol and her were the only two prisoners in this place.

In another heartbeat, Ynya stood outside her sister's cage. Synol still stared with rapt amazement at her hair.

"It's okay, Synol, I'm going to get us out of here. Scoot back so I don't burn you."

She grabbed the bars and poured heat into them, but Synol refused to move.

No matter, she was probably in shock.

Ynya's heart thundered in her chest. *Lub dub. Lub dub. Lub dub.*

She bent the bars, her vision pure red as she parted them.

"Ynya!" Synol finally yelled, her face still struggling to process the actions of her younger sister.

"Synol, come! We don't have much time."

Dumbly, Synol stared at her sister.

Ynya turned to look for an exit. She wondered how much longer they had until the guards arrived.

None of that mattered right now, she just needed to work in securing an exit and to make it out of here. They needed to escape, they needed to run and hide. Then, they could tear this place apart stone by stone looking for their sister.

Ynya lowered the brilliance of her hair down to just a few strands on each side. Each one still gave plenty of light, but she had burned through a lot of power in a tiny amount of time. She didn't know what was beyond the door and didn't know how much more energy she would need to help them escape.

"Synol, did you see everything when they brought us in?"

"Yes, we are on the north end of the compound. I think the third or fourth building over from the north-east corner."

"Good."

"Ynya, your ear is bleeding."

"I don't care, we need to get out of here."

Ynya came to the door and grabbed the handle. She put her good ear to the door to listen for any sounds.

Synol wasn't right behind her.

"Synol?"

Synol hadn't come with her. "We're leaving without Finny and Meki?"

A mixture of guilt and anger flashed through her mind. "We'll have to come back for them."

"But we're already here. If we leave now, the soldiers will know and they'll double up all the guards. We'll never get back in again, Ynya." Her voice cracked. "I know you want to burn down the place, but our mission, our responsibility, is to our family. We can do whatever you want to this place once we accomplish that, but for now, we need to find our sisters and get them to safety."

Ynya's anger flared, devoid of the guilt now. She whirled on her sister, crossing the two paces between them in less than a heartbeat. Her resolve peaked, she was furious and needed to take it out on someone.

Ynya grabbed her sister's upper arms. She didn't mean to hurt her, but her fingers dug into them.

"One of them is dead, Synol. You heard the Warden, one of them is dead."

"We don't know that."

"Yes we do! You heard him! They didn't find a use for her and disposed of her!"

Synol ground her teeth. "I don't care what he said. I'm not leaving this place until we find one of our sisters and verify the other's safety. He was probably lying. He wanted to get a reaction out of us. Do you think the Frost Queen would hunt down all four of us just to have us killed during testing? That bastard was trying to break us, just like this room is designed to do. I know they're both alive and I will not stop until I get them to safety."

Ynya fell to her knees, releasing her sister's arms.

Emotion welled up inside of her, a grief so deep she had no idea where it came from. The idea that one of her sisters was dead was too much to bear. Too much to handle.

No.

She pushed her emotions down deep. She had to bury them. If she allowed the grief to take over, to consume her, she would fall victim to it and she knew she wasn't climbing out of that. Should wouldn't allow herself to be a victim of her own depression. She would rise above and do what was needed.

"What are you going to do?"

Synol sighed. "We're going to get tested. Once we're back in the Pit, we'll do what we can to find them. If they were both here, then someone else in that pen would have seen them. I refuse to believe that one of them is dead, and until I see her corpse for myself. I won't believe anything out of the Warden's mouth."

Synol put out her hand, which Ynya took. "Come, sister. Let us get back to what we need to do in order to find our sisters."

Ynya struggled with what to say, with what to do. She wanted to fight. It was what drove her, it was how she reacted to unknown and uncomfortable situations – fire and fervor, with maybe a large bit of sass.

But Synol was right. This was an entirely different situation. They were trapped in the most complicated prison system they had ever heard of, and getting out would require subtlety.

While there would be a time for fighting, that was not now. At least one of their sisters was still here and acting out might cause undo harm to her.

Ynya wouldn't be able to live with herself if she did something to jeopardize her sister's safety.

Ynya frowned. She hated to admit she was wrong, so she would just not say anything for now. She grabbed Synol and shoved her farther back into the cage.

"What?"

"It's better this way. That way you don't get in trouble, either. It's better if I'm the only one that is punished for my actions, rather than both of us. Whatever they do to me, I want you to promise that you will stay the course and find our sisters."

Ynya heated up the bars again, pulling against them with all her strength to bend them back to their original shape.

Finally, she had them back roughly to where they should be and Synol was safely back in her cage.

Ynya then opened the door and yelled at the top of her lungs, "You can't contain me! I'm fire incarnate!"

Chapter Fourteen

They stitched up her ear after they captured, beat, and stabbed her once again with the silver daggers.

She was then visited by the Warden to put in her new bronze earring.

"Tsk, tsk, tsk. I had high hopes for you, but I never thought you would try to escape. Though I am a bit disappointed that you hadn't tried to take your sister with you."

Ynya spat at him, but missed. "I tried, but she refused to come, heated up her bars and everything but she said it wasn't worth it."

He smiled back with that crooked cocky smile of his. "She's a smart one. You would do well to follow her lead, but if I'm going to be perfectly honest, I don't mind you trying to break out. The occasional breakout attempt reminds the other prisoners that they're here for as long as we need them."

He paused, holding the earring apparatus. "In fact, it's probably a good test for my soldiers to learn where we're getting lax. Don't worry, the soldiers that were supposed to be monitoring the chamber for movement have been punished and will not be making that mistake again, so I thank you for bringing attention to me the issues I had in my ranks."

"I'll be happy to show you more."

He smiled, and shook the earring apparatus again in her face. "Oh, I don't think you will. You see, the silver earrings we put in you are special, of course. They wouldn't be able to void your magic otherwise, but they are cheap and plentiful enough that we can easily afford to put them into every prisoner. But some of you," he tugged on his earlobe to punctuate the point, "get the bright idea to think for yourself. I understand and commend that to some extent, especially harming yourself to get your magic back. I have respect for that sort of dedication, I really do."

He stopped monologuing to cough to the side. He sounded sick, with a deep rattle in his throat that made Ynya hope he would just fall over dead there in front of her.

He spat something yellow and slimy onto the ground before continuing. "But these bronze earrings are unique. You see," he held the loop closer for her to see. "Like this, they are an open circuit of pure energy. The magic is trapped inside, unable to move, so it lays dormant. But once this is closed, the energy whirls round and round. As long as there is human flesh for it to contact and dump off the excess heat and magic, it will be a little warm to the touch but not unbearable. In fact," He paused and cocked his head to the side, "I do think you might find the extra heat pleasant.

"But if you should attempt to pull this one out, it will put off a chain reaction so violent, that it will take off your hand, your arm, and there have been a few cases where half of the patient's head came off with it."

Ynya gulped. "A few?"

He grinned and waggled his eyebrows. "Oh, like nine in

ten patients. So you are welcome to take the chance, but I can guarantee that you will lose your hand and arm for sure. Past that, I don't rightly know. I guess it matters how fast you pull it from your ear. But just in case you thought you were going to get lucky, I leave you with one last thing."

The Warden grabbed another unclosed loop from the table. "When I'm done here, I'll be putting this loop into your sister's ear. These two are very special, and highly dangerous, too. If one goes off, the other will detonate at the exact same moment.

"So you might feel lucky. You might feel like you are the one in ten who won't lose her head, but do you feel like your sister will be able to pull it from her ear at the same time?"

Ynya was quiet while he fitted the new bronze earring. She would have to find another way around the magic inhibitors.

EVERYTHING HURT.

Ynya hadn't understood what it truly meant for every part of her body to hurt, but now she was experiencing it.

The "testing," as they called it, consisted of a series of injections into her arm that did one of two things.

Either it did nothing, and caused an immense amount of pain.

Or it did something, and caused even more pain.

After each injection, three scientists surrounded her and measured things like her temperature, eyes, ears, and tongue. They poked her skin with other needles, checking to see if something small injected would react to whatever was being tested.

Each test took roughly three hours. When the injection

finally ran its course, and the same three scientists determined that her body was back to normal, the tests started again.

Each one was different, but somehow worse, than the last. One sprouted boils across her skin, another caused blindness, and another removed her ability to taste. One made her heat up so much she thought she was going to burn, which was the oddest feeling she had ever had because she was normally completely immune to fire.

The worst one was when they lit a small candle and burned her hair. It was only a part of a couple strands, and it was actually the least painful of all the tests, but it terrified her nonetheless. She'd always prided herself on her long, curly red hair, and the ability to light it up when she needed to.

Her hair was such an integral part of who she was, a unique, tangled, and fiery mass of red, that watching a part of her affected by fire for the first time in her life scared her to her toes.

Ynya couldn't hold back the tears. She'd lost a part of herself, and for a while after that she worried that whatever they were doing to her would permanently alter who she was.

Her mind went down a path it had never gone before. *What if I have to live the rest of my life without magic?* She'd spent so long assuming it was such an integral part of who she was. *Would I be the same without it?*

Does magic define who you are, or only enhance? Who would I be if I didn't have access to that heat?

I'd be like everyone else.

She calmed down later when they tried another concoction that chilled her entire body. They tried the flame test on her hair once again and it was immune to fire.

That gave her hope. At least she thought it was hope.

One test in particular got the scientists all in a tizzy as they tried to assess the results. All three of them spoke in a foreign language, so Ynya wasn't able to understand exactly what they said. She did understand that they were abnormally agitated about something. They tried the same concoction on her three times in a row. Each time it gave her a pleasantly warm feeling through her body, almost like she was in a good mood.

It disconcerted Ynya – being strapped to a table and having a strange sense of peace come over her as three scientists buzzed about like bees on a spring flower.

At least this last one seemed to go by fast, because they repeated the test on her three times in a far shorter window than they normally did.

So rather than worry about what they tested her for, Ynya enjoyed the pleasant feelings, relishing them as the scientists continued to buzz about her. The world could just keep spinning around while she lay there, euphoric and alone.

She wondered how Synol fared through all the tests. Ynya would never forget that steely gaze Synol gave her when she refused to come out of her cage. Synol was right at that moment, Ynya had to admit that.

Smoke, not fire.

The euphoric moment wore off and everything returned to normal. The buzzing stopped and the overall pains and aches of her last few abuses came back with a vengeance.

They released her, but not before sending her back to the old woman to inscribe her with more ordinals up the inside of her arm and onto her shoulder.

Ynya was now one of them, branded for life.

Chapter Fifteen

"Ynya!" Synol limped toward her sister as soon as she entered the Pit. It was early morning again. Ynya realized had no sense of time during the testing. *Did I lose a whole day? Two?*

"Synol, are you okay?"

Synol frowned at her leg. "It's nothing. It'll heal eventually."

Ynya wanted to press further, but Synol pulled her shirt sleeve up to show the edge of her ordinals. They only came halfway up her upper arm.

Ynya frowned, feeling like she was the oddball once again in the family. She pulled back her shirt over her shoulder to show the edge of the numbers.

Synol gasped, then grabbed her sister in a massive bear hug. "It's okay, little sister. We will find our family and figure out how to get out of here, and then we will all go back to Marsfjord and rebuild the whole place. If we have to, I will pick up the entire town and move it out to the middle of the ocean where we won't be bothered ever again by the Frost Queen or her armies."

Ynya wanted to cry, she knew this was the time to do so, but there was something inside her that refused. A hardness growing slowly over time that refused to succumb.

Yes, she'd been terrified when they burned her hair, but that was a very personal, very intimate part of her that hadn't been breached until now. It was akin to learning that your mother and father were not infallible, that they made mistakes too. It was like learning about a woman's mooncycle. Something fundamental about her life had changed in that moment, that could never be taken back.

She had faced the realities of not ever having magic again and survived.

But this hardness was just that. A hardness against all the atrocities she'd experienced up to this point. There was no point crying because the Frost Queen was a ruthless bitch who tortured children to create her armies. There was no point in worrying about any of that because it was just life around here.

Worrying was wasted energy. What Ynya needed was focused effort.

She couldn't control what the Frost Queen and her minions did, but she could control what she did, and any time wasted worrying about them, or feeling sorry for herself or her sister was time not working on a solution to their problems.

Ynya pulled away, grabbing Synol by the arms. "We need a plan."

Synol stopped, her mouth open slightly as her eyes searched Ynya's for what she meant.

"I mean it. We keep feeling sorry for ourselves, or keep feeling like life is horrible, but we aren't any closer to escaping this place."

Synol pursed her lips. "I...agree, actually. It's what I've been saying since we got here, we need to observe—"

"No, not observe, we need to test, we need to test again." She grabbed the earring from her ear, holding it out. "I assume he told you about what this does?"

Synol's face lost what little color it had, but she nodded. "You know he could have lied about the exploding part?"

Ynya shrugged. "Doesn't matter if he's telling the truth or not. Our reality is that we don't have magic, so that is how we plan. Take him down without magic.

"It also means that we have him on the defensive right now. You observe, but I'm going to keep testing for weak spots. I'm done being told what to do. If we keep pushing them, eventually they are going to make a mistake, and we already know that they are so complacent that they leave prisoners alone in cages that can easily be escaped from by simple fire mages.

"Above all, I just want to move forward with the plan to find our sisters. This has gone on long enough."

Synol released Ynya finally. "I'm with you, but we need to be careful and not show everything we have right out of the gate. If we discover a weak point, we need to keep it to ourselves. Exposing that one with the cages means we can't use that anymore, you understand?"

Ynya nodded. "I do. I will do my best to find the weak points but not expose them."

"So, where do you think we should start?" Synol asked, looking around the Pit.

Ynya chuckled.

"What?"

"I was going to ask you the same thing."

Synol put her hands on her hips. Well, one of us needs to be in charge."

Ynya took Synol's hand. "I think it should be you. You have the more level head. I have plenty of spitfire, but what we need right now is a cooler temperament."

Synol nodded. "Fine, but you are in charge of the next big predicament we come to."

"Deal."

Synol looked around. "I think we need to find Joanne and that boy again and see if we can start making friends in this place."

Chapter Sixteen

The girls were not able to find Joanne after looking through The Pit, but they did find Tyrain huddled in a corner of the northern fence. He didn't look up when they approached him, but he had a look in his eye that told Ynya he had just gone through something horrible.

"Tyrain, are you okay?"

When he didn't respond to her voice, she knelt down, putting her hand on his shoulder. "Tyrain?"

He jumped, like he hadn't know they were there. His eyes went wide, with a wild look to them. He retreated back toward the wall, cowering from her touch.

Synol asked Ynya to move so she could get to the boy.

"Tyrain." Synol knelt down an arm's distance away. "Did they take you Tyrain?"

He looked at her for a moment, his eyes not focusing. She kept her distance but put on a warm, motherly smile. Eventually, his gaze focused and he nodded, but it was still a wild, untamed nod, like you would get from a young child.

"Okay. Do you know if they took Joanne? Did they take you and Joanne to the same place?"

He glanced behind him, looking at the buildings to the north. He pointed at a door four buildings down. "First Enlightenment."

The girls shared a look.

Synol put her hand out, palm up, but kept her distance from him, allowing him to make the first move. "Do you need help standing?"

He picked up his hand, almost by rote, but then stopped. "No. Actually, I just want to sit here."

Synol retracted her hand. "That is fine. Is it okay if I sit here with you?"

He nodded, then glanced up at Ynya. "They took her. I heard her scream. I screamed too. They were not nice."

Ynya balled her fists. "I knew it."

"If you can tell us anything about what goes on in there, it might help us know how to help you and Joanne once she comes out."

He nodded, then glanced back at the building. "They make you pray."

"You pray?"

"Yes, but they strip you down to nothing and put you in a cold room so you start to shiver, and if you pray to the Frost Queen they sprinkle warm water on your back."

"What the hell?"

"Is that all?"

"No. If you refuse to prey they throw ice at you until you kneel in the water."

"Gods Below," Synol said. "It's okay if you prayed, Tyrain. It is. They shouldn't have made you do that, but you have to do what will keep you alive. There is no shame in keeping yourself alive."

"Joanne wouldn't pray. I heard her in the room next to mine. She refused, and they threw ice. She screamed louder, and they threw more ice, and when they ran out of ice they shut the door to let her freeze. Eventually she stopped screaming, but I know she was still alive because she spoke to me through the walls. She told me to get out of there. She told me to do what they say and she would come see me once she got out."

Ynya tugged on Synol's dress, pulling her away.

She kept her voice low. "Do you think they are going to let her out of there anytime soon?"

Synol glanced back at the boy but shook her head. "I'd be surprised if they did until she broke. Letting her out now might be easy."

She knelt back in front of the boy. "Tyrain, Joanne mentioned to us the last time we saw her that she has some friends here. Friends who get to work outside of The Pit sometimes?"

He nodded. "Thore and Gustav?"

"Yes, those are the ones. Do you know if they are in The Pit right now or are they out doing their jobs?"

The boy shook his head. "Thore works the walls and lives in the barracks. He's one of the guards but treats us well when he can. Gustave works in the bellower and lives here with his family. You can find them all closer to the bell tower. He has no hair and is big from using that large mallet to ring the bells. They also feed him plenty of food that he shares with his family when he can. He might actually be off-shift right now."

The sisters shared a look.

Ynya nodded. "I'll talk to him and see what I can get. You'll be okay here?"

Synol shooed Ynya away.

"GUSTAVE?" THE MAN WAS PRETTY EASY TO RECOGNIZE. He was a full foot taller than everyone else with a shaved head and thick, corded muscles under his thick skin. He wore cutoff pants and sandals, but no shirt.

Ynya paused a moment to take in how huge his chest was when he turned toward the sound of his name.

"Yes?"

Her gaze lingered on his bulging muscles.

What is wrong with me?

She shook her head to clear the haze that had suddenly overtaken her mind.

"My name is Ynya, I'm a friend of Joanne."

The burly man excused himself from his group of people and walked over to her. "Oh yeah. How is she doing?"

Ynya's mind focused. "She, uh, she's being Enlightened right now."

His face softened and took on a concerned expression. "I'm sorry to hear that."

Ynya nodded, but a hundred questions burned in her head. "Can you tell me what goes on in there?" She glanced at his ordinals, ending just past his elbow. She noticed the strange symbols at the end, something she hadn't seen yet.

He followed her gaze. "It's because I only have the two abilities."

"What?"

"I see you're looking at my Ordinals." He pointed to his elbow. "Here is the date and my unique identifier. Here are the ordinals for my testing. As you can see, they only go to my elbow. The ones after signify I've completed the First and Second Enlightenments."

Ynya noticed that his skin had fully healed over from the invasive tattoo method, while hers was still raw and painful. "How long has it been?"

He held out his wrist, indicating the first few numbers. "Sixteen years. I came here when I was eight."

Ynya gasped. "You've been here as long as I've been alive."

A strange silence grew between them, but it wasn't uncomfortable, just reflective.

He glanced over his shoulder and placed his massive hand on her small back. "Come, let's go over here where there are fewer ears."

They walked a dozen paces away. "The First Enlightenment is all about them showing that they have absolute control over you. It's about breaking you down, leaving you raw and exposed. It's painful, both mentally and physically."

He glanced around once more.

"The Second Enlightenment is all about programming you to obey the Frost Queen. All the guards you see out there, or anyone with a job outside of The Pit completed that second training. Many of those that are in here have only been through the First. They will only take those that have broken completely to become guards or beyond."

"Skarmyord." Ynya replied.

He nodded. "Or worse."

"So, what about you?"

He grinned, and when he did, her heart melted. She wanted to jump into his massive arms and ask him to carry her around all day.

What is wrong with me?

"I have two abilities." He pointed to his bicep as large as Ynya's head. "Firstly, I have a lot of strength. You should have seen me as an eight year old when I first bloomed. I was almost this muscled but in a small package. I was pretty odd looking."

She nodded, suppressing an image that popped into her head. She couldn't stop looking at how huge his muscles were.

"My second ability is charisma."

Something broke inside her mind, and suddenly she wasn't fascinated by his muscles anymore. She looked up at his face, hoping she didn't get lost in his dark brown eyes again. She was a little disappointed when she wasn't.

"Sorry, I have to concentrate really hard to turn it off, and I can only do it for one or two people at a time."

"What do you mean?"

His face flushed. "I accidentally spelled you. It's hard for me because it's on by default and I have to work to turn it off when I speak to people."

She finally realized what he was talking about. She had been so wrapped up in how thick his body was, or how dream-like his eyes were that she hadn't realized it was magic.

Magic.

"Wait, how are you able to do magic?" She looked at his ear and realized he didn't have any earring, though she did see the lingering scar from a hole long ago.

"Anyone who survives the first two Enlightenments can have their earrings taken out." He frowned as he looked at her stitched-up earlobe. "I see you tried ripping it out?"

She nodded.

He put a hand on her shoulder. "It's okay. It happens a few times a year, usually in the middle of The Pit. I think they prefer when prisoners do that so they can make a big spectacle of taking them down and putting in the new one. But yes, if you make it through both Enlightenments, you can have your earring taken out, but it's not an easy proposition."

"What do you mean?" This was the main reason she had come here, to learn how the Enlightenments worked.

He sighed like he had a heavy load on him. It was a deep, mournful sigh filled with regret and pain.

"Depending on how many skills you have, you either become a soldier, perform duties around the camp, or are sent to train to be a Skarmyord. It all depends on how many abilities you have, and what they are. If they have need of someone specific, they will take them for that job." He paused. "Rumor is that if you have frost magic of any type the Queen takes you for herself. Why, I don't know."

His eyes glanced down to the dozens of ordinals adorning her arm and peeking out her dress's shoulder. He winced for a second but then cleared his face.

"It's okay, I know I have a lot."

He nodded, clearly trying to avoid discussing it further. "I lucked out in that my charisma was so powerful, pretty much everyone just let me go as soon as I was put into any situation that involved Enlightenments."

He held up his arm again. "I really didn't have to do anything that anyone else has gone through here because as soon as they strapped me down into the chair and removed the earring to Enlighten me, they all felt bad for me and would just write down in their documents that I passed."

Ynya snorted, even though her brain told her it wasn't funny that he hadn't endured torture. "So you just flirted with everyone and got yourself into a job banging on bells?"

He shrugged. "It's what I do best, so here I am."

He turned to look back at the group of people he was with. "My family hasn't fared as well as I have, though. My older sister was taken away a long time ago and I've never seen her since. I'm pretty sure she was turned into Skarmyord."

He pointed. "My mother and father adopted my sister and I when we were young. Neither of them have magic, but they won't let them out. Luckily, they haven't had to endure most of the torture they do to the people here, and I'm able to bring them extra food and clothes to keep them healthy."

His countenance darkened as he looked at a young woman sitting on the ground between his parents. She held onto each of them with one hand.

"She hasn't fared very well, though. My younger sister went into Skarmyord training, she had almost as many ordinals as you have in fact, but after a year, she was dumped back into The Pit like that. She's never spoken since, and sucks on her toes when she's scared. It's like she's reverted to being an infant again."

Ynya's heart sunk as she looked at the girl who looked to be about Synol's age.

Above them, the bells chimed. Time for an announcement.

Chapter Seventeen

❧❀❧

"2201." The Translator stood over her, holding a light in front of her eyes. "Can you hear me?"

She grunted in the affirmative.

"I can't say how disappointed I am with you, 2201. I thought we had an understanding about unleashing your abilities."

She knew what she needed to say to this. She had been taught.

"I have no abilities but what the Frost Queen grants me. All my abilities serve Her. I am a vessel, filled but not overflowing with the Concordance. Through her, I will be made glorious, and spend eternity in Her service. Glory to our Queen."

He pursed his lips. "Yes, well, I'm glad to hear you memorized that properly, but I'm more concerned with how you unleashed your winds in here. Did She tell you to unleash the winds?"

"No, the voice told me to. I tried to ignore her, as I was

trained, but the pain allowed her to come forth. I couldn't keep her from taking over. She was very insistent."

"Ahh." He nodded, clucking his tongue. "This is all-too common for those of you who are put through the Enlightenments so quickly. It is unfortunate, but I did need you sooner rather than later. I wish there were a better way, but time waits for no one. With your abilities, I couldn't pass up the chance to get you into my chair sooner."

She didn't reply. She didn't know if she was supposed to, so she remained silent.

"Well, all that said, I want you to remember your training. Remember the Enlightenments and how to keep your old voice down. Remember that you are part of something grand now and you must leave your old life behind."

<<*Ynya will come for you*>> the voice told her.

"Of course, if you aren't able to keep your mind from wandering, I might have to take you back to the Second Enlightenment for more conditioning. You wouldn't want that, now, would you?"

She shook her head. She had spent weeks going through the Enlightenments before the Translator had come for her. Weeks of torture and training. Weeks to tell her that her old life was behind her. No one came to help her, but if she gave herself over wholly to Her, then she would be taken care of. She would be wrapped in Her frigid embrace and learn to love the frost.

<<*Synol will come for you.*>>

She hadn't broken, not really, but three solid weeks of relentless torture had been enough to convince her to leave her past self behind.

At least some of the time.

<<*I never left you, and I never will.*>>

"Well, I still have to take precautions of my own if I'm going to ensure any sort of result out of this next serum. I'm going to have to sedate you so that we don't have any more of your outbursts, do you understand? Normally, I wouldn't want to do this because it might affect the end result, but like I said, compromises needed to be made in this case."

She nodded. She understood.

She had destroyed his lab, and all of his serums. For an entire day he had to scramble and get everything fixed in the lab before he could begin his experiments on her again.

<<*I kept him from hurting you again. It was only one day, but he hasn't hurt you in that time.*>>

"Well, then. We should begin."

The Translator pulled a needle from his pocket and fiddled with it for a moment, then stuck it into her arm and plunged the purple liquid in.

There was no pain, not this time. She ignored pain, looked past it. She focused on Her in all things. She protected 2201, and kept her from failing. She was everything. She was the Frost Queen, and the Frost Queen was She.

No other voices bothered her as the serum took hold and plunged her into the darkness.

"1267071302! Time for your First Enlightenment!"

Ynya looked down at her arm, reading the numbers that had just been called out. She would never get used to being called by a number, it was demeaning and dehumanizing.

Which is why they do it.

She looked around at the hundreds of faces that didn't bother looking up. Maybe you did get used to it after a while.

She shuddered at the thought of being here so long that she wouldn't think of her name anymore.

Gustave frowned. "You better go."

Ynya nodded. "Thank you for your help. I guess I will see first-hand what the First Enlightenment is all about."

His large eyebrows furrowed. "Do you want me to talk to the guards? I might be able to keep them at bay for a while if you want."

She shook her head. "No. Thank you, though. I think I can handle it. I want to know what everyone else is being put through."

Gustave's face was deep with worry, but he nodded. "I have heard of people resisting. Keep your mind focused on something positive."

"1267071302! Last chance!"

Ynya raised her arm and yelled. "I'm coming!"

She turned to face the guard, but as she did, she caught sight of Synol, who was mid-stride through the pen. Behind her was Tyrain. He had more color in his face now.

She smiled at them, and raised a hand, despite the exasperated, terrified expression on her sister's face.

"I love you." She mouthed the words, then turned toward the guards.

~

IT WAS AN HOUR LATER WHEN THE DOOR FINALLY OPENED to the small wooden cell.

"Ynya Oblique, so nice to meet you once again." The man in red, the Warden of this place sauntered in with a flourish. "I hope you have been enjoying our accommodations."

She growled. "You tie me up in a wooden room with

nothing to do. I think I'd rather have the ice water treatment I keep hearing about. Sounds refreshing."

He grabbed the chair on the other side of the table and sat down, crossing one long spindly leg over the other.

"Is that so? Well, I'm sure that can be arranged." He turned toward the guard at the door. "Please ensure that 1301 receives the ice treatment."

"Yes, sir."

Ynya's blood flash-boiled at her sister's number. She tried to stand up from her chair, but the restraints about her wrists and ankles held her down. "You can't do that to her!"

"Oh, but I can. You see, I can tell a lot about people. I have a feeling that whatever physical torture I put you through isn't going to be very effective. No, I need to do something much more subtle to you."

Ynya wanted to jump across the table and bite the man's nose off. She pulled against her chair once again, but it was bolted to the floor and refused to budge.

He smiled, a crooked, primeval look just dripping with malice and humor. "That's the spirit I need to break, right there. You love your sisters quite a bit, don't you?"

He snapped his fingers and a female guard came in holding two objects.

One was a book, the other was a hair.

A red hair.

Chapter Eighteen

"2201? 2201, are you still with me?"

She awoke with a gasp. Her lungs burned for air, her head pounded, and the bottom half of her body was numb.

<<*He almost killed you*>> The voice was back.

"Well, that was quite exciting, I must say. Nearly lost you there."

The Translator dabbed at his forehead with a handkerchief, wicking away the beads of sweat that adorned his pale grey skin.

<<*He is nervous about almost killing you.*>>

"I nearly died?"

He looked at her with a quizzical expression. "Uh, yes. Yes, you did, but that is no matter. Glory to the Frost Queen if we give our lives."

He gave her a half-hearted smile. "Nothing to worry about. While there may have been some complications with the dosage, the initial testing I was able to perform on you during those moments was quite promising."

"Promising?"

"Oh yes." He grabbed a pad of paper and scanned over it. "Your body took to the serum quite well, I must say. Better than anyone else I've seen up to this point, in fact. It's quite remarkable that your mind is this sharp following the initial testing as well, though I do have to worry if your brain cut off secondary functions in order to ensure survival of primary, so that might explain why you are so lucid now when previous tests showed noticeable degradation."

He squinted at something on the paper then looked up and scanned her ordinals. "In fact, you have near-perfect traits for what I'm working on, but we still need to keep your magic under control next time I begin the full treatments."

<<*He's going to change you into a monster.*>>

He pulled a tube from under her arm, scrutinized it, and tossed it to the side.

"I'm going to need more tubing, and double these restraints for the next pass. I don't think we're going to get another chance at this."

In the back, a female assistant replied. "Yes, sir," then marched out of the room.

The Translator stood, pacing back and forth, mumbling numbers and words to himself.

2201 looked around the room. It was still destroyed from the last experiments. Broken tables and chairs lined the walls. The middle was cleared of the debris as well as two doors. One door led to the hallway, while the other to a room. Two soldiers fitted glass into a cutout on that wall.

"What is the window for?"

"Huh?" The Translator looked up. "Oh, it's just another observation room, should I ever get more than one patient in here. It will allow me to work on multiples at once."

A thought percolated in her mind, but not from the voice. It was a memory, something she had seen with her own eyes.

A girl with red hair had been in that room.

She had screamed. She cried and begged to be let go.

She had locked eyes with her and hadn't taken her gaze from 2201 the entire time.

Everything had gone white.

2201 remembered them replacing the window before.

<<*For the second time.*>>

"You did have multiple patients. You had my sister. Is she still here? I would like to leave with her."

The Translator yelled for his assistant, and soon they injected her arm with more sedative.

As the drug worked through her system and mingled with her blood, she remembered the red curly hair. She remembered the cries of anguish. She remembered her voice, young and sweet, and full of emotion.

The girl had called 2201 something.

Something other than 2201.

"What are those?" Ynya panicked, seeing the red hair placed on the wooden desk before her. "Whose is that?"

The Warden picked up the hair with two fingers, holding the strand between them. "Oh, this? This is one of your sister's."

Ynya pulled against her restraints once again. "Whose? Whose is it? Finny? Meki? It's too curly for Synol! Tell me!"

He smiled and let go of the thin hair. It fell, alighting on the book where he brushed it off and back to the table.

"Oh, Ynya. There seems to be a gross misconception that

you are somehow in control. You seem to think that if you yell at me more, or demand that I give you something, that I will just give it to you."

He picked up the hair once again. "I don't have to give you anything I don't want to, and right now, I have no desire whatsoever to give you any information."

He turned, holding the hair out. "Take this to the sister's room, we will need it for later."

"Yes, sir."

The guard left with the single hair.

Ynya fumed. In her struggles, the manacle had cut into her wrist. It was already raw from the Ordinations and it now bled. Blood dripped down the chair and onto the floor.

The Warden picked up the book and flipped it open. It was another of the registration books that Ynya and Synol found earlier.

"Do you know what this one is from?"

Ynya didn't reply.

He snapped his fingers.

Two guards moved like the wind through the doorway, grabbed her head with a harness, and pulled it back so she looked straight up.

One grabbed a skin of water and held it up to her mouth.

"I asked you a question, but if you are not going to answer me, then I will have to assume the only reason is that you have a mouth full of water that prevents you from speaking."

Ynya smiled.

"I thought you weren't going to torture me? I thought that you were going to use other methods to break me."

He chuckled for a long while, which turned into cough like it had before. After he caught his breath, he snapped, waving his hands around. The guards let go of Ynya's head and left the room.

"Oh, you are going to be so much fun, aren't you? Fine, but I expect answers, or I will have to show you something that is quite...unpleasant."

She looked at the book. Given the strange handwriting and the ledger being upside down, she couldn't quite make out what the words were. "It's a ledger from the Hall of Records."

"Very good, but it's not the one with you and your sisters, oh no. This one is much older."

"How old?"

He picked up the book, showing her the spine.

"Seventy years ago?"

He placed the ledger back down on the table and spun it around.

"As you can see, there are two names on this that might interest you. The handwriting is a little archaic, but we've since improved our teaching methods to ensure we're not using obscure dialects anymore. If you read carefully, however, you might notice you recognize a few words."

Ynya read over the page. Much of it was illegible, but three words stuck out, arranged over the course of two names.

"Talia Oblique and Nora Oblique?"

Chapter Nineteen

They dumped her back into the Pit as the 20th bell rang.

"Ynya?" Gustave pushed through the crowd with Tyrain in tow.

"Have you seen Synol?" She asked, picking herself off the ground.

Gustave shook his head. "I'm sorry, no. I spoke with her for a little while after they took you away but then they came for her, too."

"He tried to talk to the guards, but they wouldn't listen to him." Tyrain interjected.

Ynya looked around. "What about Joanne?"

Both men looked dumbly at her.

"Dammit. Is there anything we can do?"

"Sorry, there isn't anything. What did they do to you?"

Ynya scowled and paced along the northern edge of the Pit. She studied each door in hopes of obtaining any bit of information about where Synol was.

"Ynya?"

She whirled on Gustave, how dare he–

No. It's not his fault.

She stopped pacing, willing herself to not move. "I spoke to the Warden while chained to a table. He threatened me a couple times, showed me a single strand of red hair, and some names in a book. That's all he did to me for hours. He didn't hit me, burn me, throw anything at me. He didn't do anything to me!"

As she spoke, rage built up in her mind once again. Ynya was mad that he hadn't tortured her. She worried that anything she had said or admitted to him in that session had been meted out on her sister in her stead.

Ynya couldn't bear knowing that Synol had suffered instead of her. The thought was almost too much to handle. Not knowing what was going on was the worst part. If they had just tortured her, then she would have been able to handle it, but the way things were going, she didn't know what she would do...

"Ynya." Gustave grabbed her by the shoulders and stopped her pacing. His massive hands were warm on her cool skin. They felt welcoming and caring.

Part of her wanted to ask him to pull her in, to hug her, and keep her warm. She missed someone big and warm to hold her and tell her everything was going to be alright. She missed her father.

The other part wanted to push him away, tell him to never touch her like that again.

She split her decisions down the middle. She stopped and stared at him.

"What?"

"Pacing and making fists isn't going to do any good for Synol right now. Did the Warden indicate she was anywhere specific?"

Her mind stopped whirling out of control from the question. Had the Warden said anything of value? He had about her mother, but that was too much to worry about for now. She needed to focus on Synol.

She shook her head. "No, I don't think so."

"That's a start. It's not much, but it's something. We don't know where she is."

The bells chimed for attention.

"1267071302! Time for your Enlightenment!"

"You have got to be kidding me, I just got back here."

Gustave let go of her. "It's one of the tactics they use. Sleep deprivation and continually calling you. They are trying to make sure you stop having any identity other than what they give you."

Ynya balled her fists once again. "Well, then I'll make sure to hold on to it."

She marched forward, identifying herself to the guards once again.

As they took her from the Pit, she glanced back to Gustave and Tyrain. They watched her with sorrowful looks on their faces.

The soldiers led her past two doors and told her stand just outside of one.

A door opened to the side and two guards stepped out with Synol between them.

Synol limped out. A soldier to either side helped keep the weight off her right leg. Her matted hair clung to her face and shoulders. She had a bruised eye and a cut along her jaw.

Ynya's heart sunk and she opened her mouth to yell. As she did, a gloved hand grabbed her from behind and pulled her through the door.

The hand cut off her voice before she could say anything.

The door shut, plunging Ynya's world into darkness.

They wrestled her into manacles once again, and replaced the glove with a ball stuffed in her mouth that prevented her from vocalizing anything but grunts and groans.

Ynya had to be careful to not struggle too much, because she was barely able to breathe.

Finally, a lit torch returned the light.

The Warden sat across from her once again.

Two blood-stained rags lay at his feet. He methodically wiped four speckles of blood from his face before looking up.

"Fancy meeting you here, Ynya. You keep making friends every time you leave, so we'll be sure to learn those names and bring them in for questioning."

He finished with the rag and tossed it on the floor with the rest.

She glared at the pile.

He followed her gaze. "Oh yes, that would be Synol's blood, of course. She doesn't seem to be able to withstand my interrogation techniques very well and certainly has a lot to say."

He stuck a finger in his ear and pulled out a rolled-up bunch of wool. "This helps, though. Constant screaming in your ears can really wear you down, don't you think? One should really worry about their mental health in a place like this."

He pulled a ball of wool from his other ear and dropped them both on the floor. "You know what I love to hear though? Laughter. And you know what they say about laughter, Ynya?"

He turned and placed his palm upright behind him, waiting for the guards to hand him something. "They say that laughter is the best medicine."

He showed her the two large black feathers in his hand.

"Now I don't know where they came up with the phrase, because honestly, it doesn't sound right to me. I would think healing magic is the best medicine, but what do I know? I torture people for a living, so maybe I'm wrong."

"These were supposedly left by the Raven herself after a particularly bloody night here at the compound." He struck a pose, with one hand on his hip and another on his chin. "Though it does bring up a question. If I am wrong, I suppose I will need to test my theory, right? I should test it until I have enough data to support my new hypothesis."

He held his arms out and two soldiers helped him out of his red leather jacket. "I won't be needing that for now. No point in wearing red leather if you're not going to use it for hiding blood, right?"

He wiggled the feather in his right hand at Ynya. "Prepare her."

Two soldiers stepped forward, grabbing her and wrenching her body straight while also doing the same to the chair.

Before Ynya knew it, she was tied to a stretcher.

They flipped it over on some unseen hinge, suspending her by the wrists and ankles with the stretcher to her back. They hoisted her into the air and hung her so she faced downward parallel to the ground.

The Warden approached her.

Ynya hung above him, the ball gag still in her mouth.

"It's good you wear such thin dresses. It means I can get to your underarms easier this way." He wiggled the feather at her again. "Oh, and your neck and feet. Yes, Ynya. I think we're going to get a lot of data for my new hypothesis."

Chapter Twenty

They put her back into the Pit.

Instead of storming in like she did last time, she walked carefully, arms folded. She took slow, methodical steps, like a mouse surveying her new environment for the first time.

"Ynya?"

She flinched.

"Ynya?" It was Gustave.

She turned to him, an uncontrollable shake in her jaw starting up the second she saw him.

She scanned his body. He seemed unhurt from what she could see.

She noticed Tyrain missing, and tried to open her mouth to speak, but words refused to come.

Ynya was too open, too raw and exposed. She wanted to hide, curl up, and pretend like the last two hours didn't happen.

The Warden hadn't hurt her physically, at least not directly.

Her lungs burned and her jaw throbbed from the gag she'd bit down on repeatedly. She'd spent an hour vacillating between biting down and opening up enough to get air into her lungs.

She'd rather have been punched in the stomach for two hours.

Finally, the words came. "Where is he? Where is Tyrain?"

The large man's face grew sullen. "They took him away. I tried to stop the guards but they wouldn't listen to me this time."

Ynya nodded. "It's because they know I care for him. They are going to take you at some point, too. Anyone in this place that I interact with, they're going to take. It's how he's going to torture me. Instead of hitting or cutting me, he's going to harm everyone I love. He's going to keep me up all night laughing, or enjoying a nice meal while my sister is in the next room having needles stuck in her."

Her body shivered. It started in the base of her skull and quickly spread through her whole body. Ynya couldn't stop it, couldn't control it. Her hands and feet shook so much that she wasn't able to keep herself standing properly.

She fell, but not to the ground.

Gustave's hands were there, holding her up. Those large, warm hands that never hurt her. Never hurt her sister or anyone else. Those warm hands that cared for his family, and tended to his younger sister when she came back a broken girl from her training.

Ynya was slowly becoming that girl. She was reverting. Time dripped away with every tear that fell from her eyes. Time she had spent maturing. Time she had spent learning. Time pulled away, threatening to stay away forever.

The bells chimed once again.

"No!" She pulled against his massive arms, unable to budge them. "I can't go back already. I just got here."

"1267071302! Time for your Enlightenment!"

Chapter Twenty-One

✿

She woke with a start as someone rapped her knuckles.

"You need to drink. I can't have my star student get dehydrated, you know."

Ynya struggled to focus on the man in front of her.

The Warden.

He didn't wear red anymore, he hadn't done that in a while. Right now he wore a fancy button-up shirt with ruffles and a vermillion handkerchief tied about his neck.

She sipped some of the water from the skin. It soothed her parched throat.

"Now, you know what I need to hear, don't you?"

Ynya shook her head. "I won't say it."

There were three of him, swimming in her vision. Three Wardens. Each had a slightly different hue to the others as they spiraled around each other.

"Ynya, I understand that you are young and impetuous, but you have to understand where I'm coming from in all of this."

He stood, pushing back his chair, then paced around the small interrogation room.

"I have all the time in the world to make you talk. I am not going anywhere, neither are any of the guards here. We can do this all day long. We have spells to keep us awake."

He grabbed his right ear, shaking the lobe at her. "Notice how I don't have the hoop through my ear. I can remove the hoop from your ear and you can wander freely around this compound without one too. All I have to hear are the words."

He sat down, spinning the chair around this time, and folded his arms against the back. "How warm would you be if you had access to your magic right now? How much better would life be if you could keep you, your sister, and those you care about warm? How much are you willing to endure for something that will inevitably happen?"

He pulled a deck of cards from his pocket and spread them out across the table.

"I'm going to play myself a game of solitaire. By the time I'm done, I expect that you will have something to say to me. If you don't, whatever suit I finish with last, will be one of the people you care about killed. Now, I can't bring myself to kill off that big oaf, but I heard you met his younger sister, right? The failed Skarmyord?"

Ynya held her breath.

"I'll tell you what. Your sister will be dragon, the boy will be the spike, Joanne will be the clover, and the failed Skarmyord will sub in for the fane. How does that sound? Shall we leave it up to the Gods to determine fate?"

Ynya gritted her teeth. She couldn't count how many times she wanted to jump across the table and tear him limb from limb. How many times she had dreamt about doing the same things to him as he did to her.

If only she had her magic.

But I don't. I don't have any magic, and I'm going to have to get out of this without it.

The Warden dealt the cards, then paused before playing.

"I did tell you that I'm very, very good at this game, right? In fact, one of the abilities enhanced in my Skarmyord training was that of card counting. I already know where every card in this hand is, and I will complete the whole game in less than a minute. Shall we time it?"

A violent explosion rocked the yard outside the building. The ground shook like an earthquake. Above them, timbers lurched and groaned. The interrogation room walls cracked, throwing shards of plaster through the middle of the room.

Ynya fell back as her chair buckled.

Rumbling and cracking continued as the whole building shook around them. Outside, a terrible noise raged through the camp, like a hurricane running aground.

Prisoners screamed, and soldiers shouted.

"Get her out of here," the Warden yelled.

Two guards grabbed Ynya and hoisted her to her feet. They removed the shackles and one threw her over his shoulder.

"Back to the Pit!"

As they ran outside, Ynya realized it wasn't an earthquake that hit the building.

It was wind.

A torrential gale blew throughout the entire compound. Fences bent, rocks and ice chunks flew through the air. Windborne detritus pelted Ynya's exposed skin, cutting her in a dozen places.

"Get her back! We need to head to section four!"

Just one guard escorted Ynya, while a torrential storm

raged all around them. If she could get away from this guard, she might have a chance to escape.

Escape.

The word was practically foreign to her at this point. Too long she'd been captured and toyed with by the Warden and his soldiers. Too long, she'd been a part of the system and not part of a solution.

Ynya kicked out with her knee, connecting with the man's stomach. She twisted and scraped at his face, her fingers catching soft flesh. She must have caught something because he dropped her with a scream.

"You bitch!"

He reeled for a second, which was just enough time for her to get to her feet.

Ynya ran, into the wind. The horrific gale tore at her clothes and pelted her with dirt and debris, but she closed her eyes and kept going.

The solder grabbed her foot and pulled. She toppled, hitting the ground.

"You're not getting away that easily!"

He seized her from behind, his thick arm choking her tiny neck.

The wind stopped.

Ynya opened her eyes, expecting to see the compound before her, but all she saw was a sheer wall of wind in a tube, reaching to the sky.

She was in the eye of the storm.

"You will leave her alone."

Something hit the man with a sickening crunch of bone and squish of blood. The man choking Ynya went limp and fell away.

She felt his body crumple behind her, no longer a threat.

Ynya looked into the middle of the eye, and was surprised to see a girl standing in front of her.

It was her sister.

"Finny?"

Finny's wild red hair danced on end, reaching into the sky as the violent winds surged around her. Her little hands clenched into white fists as she stared with blank eyes at Ynya.

She was terrifying and beautiful at the same time.

Ynya's heart broke. *Finny is alive!* She finally saw her sister after all this time. Her knees wouldn't support her weight anymore and she fell to the ground.

Around them, the storm raged on, people screamed, and soldiers yelled, but for one terrifying moment, the two sisters stared at each other as their red hair whipped with the wind.

Finny blinked and the eye disappeared.

The tempest overtook Ynya and pulled her into the storm, into the violent miasma of the wind.

Everything faded into nothing.

Chapter Twenty-Two

Ynya awoke to the dark. It was warm, silent, and cozy.

Too cozy.

She remembered hitting her head on the timbers last time she'd woken like this and took some time to feel around with her hands.

The ground was stone. The walls were a mixture of wood and plaster but rough, not like the smooth walls she had grown accustomed to. The walls were also incredibly close together, with barely enough room for her to sit sideways between them.

Where the hell am I?

Then she remembered.

"Finny? Finny, are you there?"

That was Finny, right? Or did I hallucinate?

Ynya didn't feel a ceiling, so she slowly stood, constantly probing out with her hands.

Every part of her body hurt. Hundreds of little cuts across her skin had scabbed over, a couple of them probably still oozed blood, but she was alive. Her hair was a tangled mess with hundreds of small objects in it.

She needed water. She needed food. She needed a bath.

The cuts across her body, while painful, were also evidence that the storm had been very real. Ynya grabbed her neck, still feeling the lingering soreness from where the soldier had choked her.

If the storm and the soldier choking me were real, was Finny real too?

Ynya stood fully erect, feeling the walls beside her. It was just wide enough to walk through with her shoulders brushing the side. *What sort of room is so narrow you could stand and walk, but only in one direction?*

It dawned on her. She was inside a wall.

She was in the space between walls inside a building.

The realization was both freeing and terrifying at the same time.

What wall in what building am I in? Why am I here? How did I get here? Did someone help me?

Ynya crouched down once again, feeling around. After a bit of crawling, she surmised she was in the wall of a room at least twelve feet across. Both ends of the wall turned in two directions.

That didn't give her much to go off of, but she could at least figure she was safe.

Voices sounded in the distance, along with clomping boots.

Ynya sat back down and pulled her knees to her chest, wrapping her arms around her legs to make herself as small as possible. She tried not to move.

Muffled, but still audible, she listened to two men come into the room. Whatever they sat on squeaked, most likely some rusty chairs. After they sat, Ynya tried to hear their conversation.

It was difficult to make out what they did while they spoke, but it sounded like they changed shoes based on the *clomp* of items dropped to the floor.

Mostly, they talked.

They spoke about repairs and lost prisoners. They spoke about the destruction and even complained about how many hours they were being forced to work to fix everything. They complained that the Warden was on a warpath and how it would take days or weeks to fix the destruction caused by the storm.

The last part made Ynya smile.

The storm was real, and there had been massive destruction throughout the encampment.

Maybe, if all of that was real, then she had actually seen Finny.

The thought warmed her heart in a way she hadn't felt in days. Knowing that one of her sisters was out there, alive, filled her with a joy she could barely contain.

Despite the pains in her body, the cuts all over her skin, and the sickening pit in her stomach from lack of nourishment, Ynya sat in the dark with a wide smile on her face.

Ynya fought the urge to cry with relief. She fought the urge to shout for joy.

She remembered she had other sisters.

She didn't know what had happened to Synol. She still didn't know where Meki was, or if she was alive or not.

She didn't know where any of her fellow prisoners were, either. Joanne hadn't been seen in days. Little Tyrain had been taken again and she worried about him handling the game the Warden liked to play with his prisoners. Finally, Ynya worried about big hulking Gustave. The Warden had said he would leave him alone, but that was before she'd gone missing.

A shudder wormed up her spine. She was missing from the camp.

That meant the Warden would be furious.

After seeing first-hand what sort of twisted tortures the man used, Ynya couldn't bear the thought that he might unleash his rage on the entire camp because she was missing.

Ynya shoved down the thought. Worrying about what one madman did was a waste of time. She was free. She would be able to help from the outside. She would be able to sneak around at night through the chaos of the repairs being done to the camp. She would help everyone else escape.

She would find Finny, and Synol, and all the rest of her friends, and get them out of here.

Then she and Synol would turn around and bury this place. The location and the people who ran it would never harm another mage ever again.

Chapter Twenty-Three

After the guards left and there was no more sound, she risked moving around again.

The first thing Ynya did was map out the area in her head. She knew one wall was about twelve feet to one side. She rounded a corner and found that the next wall was twelve feet on the other side.

Square rooms.

In the distance, she heard the soft sound of springs creaking. *Maybe I'm in their barracks?*

Loud snores confirmed her suspicions. The thought terrified her to her bones. It meant she was in the midst of her enemy.

But it was also brilliant. *Where would a prisoner go to hide? Would it be toward the soldiers, or away from them?*

It might have been the most brilliant location for her to sleep, deep in the belly of the beast, inches away from the soldiers from which she hid.

She could be side by side with them, without them even knowing it.

If only she knew how she had arrived here, then she might be able to puzzle how to get out. There was the problem of her thirst and growling belly.

Ynya kept mapping out her space. Her way became blocked and she realized she'd found a doorway. She went the other way.

She was in a wall between identical rooms. The spring sounds and snoring came from only one room.

Sleeping soldiers on one side, silence on the other.

They must be working in shifts.

That also meant she needed to be quiet in here, because there were always soldiers around.

Ynya sat and listened, silent and still as a terrified little mouse. Had she not been so still, she probably would have never noticed a slight draft of cold air against her skin. She crawled forward until she found where she had come in.

A small, low cutout in the wall led to the barracks where all the soldiers slept. An inch in front of it, probably blocking it from view, Ynya felt cool metal. *Some sort of dresser or box blocking the hole?* There was no light in the room outside, or Ynya might have found the entrance with her eyes and not by feel.

There was no way Ynya could have made it all the way into the barracks, found a hole hidden behind a metal box, and crept into this hidden space behind the walls on her own.

She had help getting here.

It's the only explanation. The question is, who helped me? Why?

She couldn't explain any of it. She hadn't befriended any of the soldiers here. In fact every last one had been incredibly professional while they dealt with her. No small talk, just orders and follow-through.

If she snuck out now and ran into the wrong guards, it would be all over. Ynya didn't know who to trust, so she needed to make sure when she did, it was safe.

She made another circuit around the walls, looking for any spot that could have been another egress to this little space, but she found none. There was only one entrance and it was apparently well-hidden. Whoever had put her here would most likely check on her at some point, and she could learn the identify of her captor then.

She hoped it was a friend, and not a foe.

Ynya dreaded the idea that someone was keeping here and she had no idea who it was.

For a moment, she wondered if this was another one of the Warden's tricks. Maybe he had put here in here to see what she would do.

She shoved out the idea. If it was a trick, there wasn't much she could do about it. If it wasn't, she didn't want to miss any opportunities that might arise out of worry that she might get punished for stepping out of line.

Ynya had nothing to lose and everything to gain by assuming this was real.

Besides, if it was all a trick, then did the Warden trick me into seeing Finny? She couldn't allow herself to believe that. She had to hold on to that faith that Finny was there.

She decided the only thing she could do was sleep. Ynya tucked herself around the corner with only her head sticking out, opposite the wall with the cutout so she could watch the opening. She wanted to see who came to visit before they saw her.

With that, she fell asleep.

Chapter Twenty-Four

Ynya awoke to some slight scraping sounds.

As long as it's not a mouse.

Luckily for her, it wasn't a mouse. Her plan to see her captor first, worked.

But it wasn't anyone she recognized.

A large head of dark curly hair pushed into the small space, followed by one of the nighttime glowing orbs.

At first, she was only able to see the back of his head as he looked away from her down the cramped little hallway. Then when he faced her, Ynya saw he was a man with incredibly dark skin.

Ynya scooted around the corner, out of sight.

The man chuckled. "I see your red hair, Ynya."

Dammit!

"It's okay, it's safe now. You can come out. I brought some food and water, and I bet you need to go to the toilet."

Her insides roiled. She needed all three really badly, especially the last one.

"We need to hurry though. The other guards will be back

from their shift shortly and will go to bed. Luckily, the Warden's issuing free vodka rations to the troops to quell the discontent from working so hard. We have about ten minutes until they are here. I couldn't break away until I had at least one drink with them, otherwise it would have looked suspicious."

It was time to make a decision. She couldn't stay here, and even if this man had plans for her, she still could move through the walls faster than he could.

She stuck her head out. "Who are you?"

She could see his features now that he faced her. His hair was even curlier than hers, but much shorter. He had a wide, burly face and broad, squished nose.

He smiled at her, showing off his large, white teeth.

She had never seen someone with such dark skin before. She knew that the farther south you went, the darker-skinned the people got because of the extra sun. Up here in the pale, cloudy north, it was all fair-skinned people who burned when the sunlight touched their skin too much.

I have to admit, he's kinda cute.

"My name is Thore. I am Joanne's friend. I work the gate to the compound."

Thore. She'd heard that name before.

"How do I know I can trust you, Thore? That's a pretty common name from up here, but you don't look like you are from the north."

He smiled again. "No, Miss. I'm from down south. I was adopted as a baby. My family found me in a basket on the edge of town after troops had killed or enslaved everyone there. They weren't sure where I came from, but they suspected my family had immigrated from farther south before the Feond went up."

Ynya frowned. There were so many stories similar to his, that she was beginning to get an idea of how the Frost Queen operated everywhere. She wondered how the Frost Queen was going to have any subjects to rule over if everyone was either in prison, or a conscripted soldier.

She crept around the corner.

"Let's get you to the bathroom first. I can sneak you over to our facility, but we'll need to do it quickly."

Thore rushed her over to the commode inside a small room at the back of the barracks. He waited outside while she did her business, just in case any other soldiers came by.

Ynya felt pretty embarrassed with a man only inches away through the door, but she had no choice. If she didn't do it now and make it back safely, then all her hiding would be for naught. Besides, her only other option was using a corner in the walls that would get her found out anyway.

Plus it was incredibly gross.

The barracks looked to be exactly what she expected from the outside. Each room was about twelve by twelve with a wall in between. Four bunks filled each room, wooden frames with metal springs underneath to suspend a straw mattress. Each barrack faced a hallway, and the smaller hallways connected to a larger corridor. The barracks were very dark, with occasionally placed orbs casting barely enough light to see without tripping, so Ynya wasn't able to get a good look at the place. She would have to sneak back out during the daytime.

The cutout to her wall hid behind a footlocker beside Thore's bed. The entrance was just small enough that the cutout fit entirely behind the metal and wood trunk. *Thore must have really squeezed to get in.*

Thore handed Ynya a small burlap bag. "There is some food in there, but you better get inside, the troops are coming."

She tossed the bag in, then paused. "Thank you for hiding me."

Her 'thank you' seemed to make him pause. "You're welcome, but please hide. I can't risk you being found out."

Ynya passed into the hole and he tossed two skins of water in behind her. "Stay silent, and I'll come get you when it's safe. I will check on you in the morning. I'll knock on my footlocker twice as I'm getting dressed. I need you to wait until everyone else has left, then knock or scrape so I know you're still there."

She nodded.

In one swift motion, he slid the footlocker in front of the cutout, leaving a small gap for air, and she was sealed up once again.

Ynya sat for a moment against the wall. Her heart beat in her chest at everything that had just happened in the last five minutes.

She still didn't know where she was exactly, or where Synol and Finny were, or how they were doing. She had no plan on how she was going to get them out. She knew very little about her mysterious rescuer.

But she had food, and she had a friend. It would have to be good enough.

As the rest of the soldiers entered into their barracks and began to strip down and change, she munched on an apple.

Ynya listened to them complain about the Warden, complain about the tireless work, and complain that there were four prisoners still missing.

Four?

She wondered who the others were.

Chapter Twenty-Five

※❖※

"2201. It's good to have you back. I hope you learned the importance of obeying and not unleashing your magic unless given express orders?"

The Translator wasn't happy with her. None of the administration at the facility were happy with her. She had caused a lot of destruction.

But it wasn't 2201. It was the other, the voice inside her. *Finny.*

Finny gave the order. Despite weeks of training to learn how to obey, 2201 wasn't able to resist when Finny took over. Finny knew words that weakened 2201.

Words like 'Ynya' or 'Synol'.

She even used a new word; 'Meki'. That was the word that allowed Finny to take over the last time, when she destroyed so much of the camp. It was the word 2201 needed to learn to resist.

The Warden insisted that she ignore the voice.

The Translator had argued with the Warden for some time, but the Warden threatened to contact to the Frost

Queen. The Translator had relented and agreed to three days of additional training.

Now she was back, and the Translator was angry.

"I learned to ignore the other voice in my head. I have blocked her entirely."

"That is good." He stepped around her with a small glow orb, shining it into her eyes. "That is very good. I am glad that you have finally learned obedience, 2201. I can't have any more outbursts like the last two times. You nearly destroyed everything we've been working so hard on. Luckily, I learned long ago to keep copies of my work at another location just in case this happened again."

She didn't reply. Replying only made things worse. Unless they asked specific questions, she was better served to listen and agree.

"Well, what's done is done. Despite our setbacks, I think that your little tantrum gave me some much-needed information regarding our serums. I see now that my dosage is simply too strong. Your body might be able to handle them, but the pain, even with your Enlightenment training, is simply too much for you to bear. Your untrained, weak mind reverts. We can't have that again. There is too much riding on this. I'm too close to lose."

He poked her arm, watching her skin spring back. He moved farther up, poking, watching, and grunting approvals.

Finally, he got to her eyes again, and alternated shining lights in them while observing.

"We need to try a slower method. Since your latest outburst killed my last two assistants, I will need some time to train up someone new. For now, I think I can handle all of this by myself."

He grabbed some bands and stretched them out a few times.

"The plan now is to inject you with a less-concentrated serum. This will allow me to monitor your dosage much more closely. If I feel the restraints can hold, I'll increase, but if you start reverting, then I will back off."

He grabbed her shoulder and squeezed. "2201, I have to warn you that another outburst like any you have shown in the past will not be pleasant for you. You have to believe me when I say this. You were slated for something quite different before I managed to intercede on your behalf. There were two of you redheads who arrived on the same day and for some reason the jackasses flagged you both for immediate disposal by Her Majesty's personal guard. Can you believe that?"

He huffed, stretching the strap across her body and latching it onto a hook on the other side.

"This isn't the first time they have mishandled lucrative subjects here at this place, but you are lucky I snagged you when I did. The alternative wouldn't have been pleasant.

"Now, we all know what that really means. It means that She wanted you two for her personal pets, to do whatever experiments she's doing in the Skarfanes, but I just couldn't pass up the opportunity. To squander such raw power is practically blasphemous, I tell you. She keeps giving me the simpletons, the weak-minded that buckle too easy, and that just won't do for what I have planned. So, I switched your records and said you were still being processed. I sent someone else in your stead. I wanted to grab your sister, but alas, I was only able to find one other redhead in the entire compound to replace, so you were it."

He grunted while he tugged on the strap, pulling it taut against her skin.

"So you have to understand, I have a very small window here to prove to Her that my experiments are worth the time investment. And I dare say, you will be well worth it when I'm able to finally finish my life's work. She would have just used you for a little while before disposing of you anyway. I say that's a waste of raw talent."

He pulled another needle from atop a desk and slid it into her arm. "I have five of these serums to get through, so we are going to take these nice and slow. This of course means you cannot move and I can't give you any food or water."

He grabbed a jar swirling with green liquid and attached the hose from that to the needle in her arm. "So 2201, are you ready to prove to Her that my experiments are worth the time? Together, we're going to make history."

Chapter Twenty-Six

꧁ꗴ꧂

As much as Ynya needed the food and water that Thore left her, she drank both skins too fast. The last few hours had been a trial in patience and slow breathing so she didn't pee herself.

While the soldiers slept on the other side of the wall, she considered sneaking out and attempting a run at the bathroom alone. But the two times she had convinced herself to do it, she heard footsteps in the hallway. After that, she distracted her mind by paying attention to the rhythm of the soldiers. Someone had restored the bells, which allowed Ynya to keep track of time.

A guard roamed the halls every half hour, day or night in the barracks. Ynya supposed that even brainwashed soldiers weren't trusted enough to ensure their own safety, and a secondary sentry was sent through to make sure things were on the up and up.

Or maybe it's just to make sure none of the soldiers are up when they're supposed to be sleeping.

The soldiers slept six hours, followed by half an hour to

wake up, change, relieve themselves, eat, and head back out for work duty.

From eavesdropping on their conversations, she learned they were also given an hour and a half after work to swing by the cantina for their ration of vodka for the night, and a little bit of time to socialize.

That meant they worked for sixteen hours straight with eight off for sleep and other functions.

Ynya also figured out that a block of rooms were all on the same schedule, and one group started their shift a bit before the block she was in, while another block farther down the building started later.

They must stagger their shifts by an hour so as to not overwhelm the kitchen, cantina, or washrooms, while still keeping most workers out moving rubble during the daylight hours. It's smart, if a little regimented. Synol would love it.

But regimented meant she would be able to time things perfectly if she needed.

"Ynya?"

"Thore?"

Their last communication had been nearly sixteen hours ago when he left for his shift. Two knocks followed her reply.

She hustled out of the confined space between the walls and hit the bathroom as fast as she could.

As much as she appreciated Thore's hiding her, Ynya needed to know more about her new supposed friend. She decided to query him while she was on the commode.

"I need to ask you some questions."

"What about?"

"Like who you are, and why you're helping me."

There was a pause before Thore spoke. "Do you have to ask this now, while you're...there?"

"Yes," Ynya growled back through the wooden door, "because we only have five minutes every day together, I want to make sure I know who is helping me. I also don't want to waste my life hiding out in a wall. I need to find my sisters and get out of here."

He sighed. "That's understandable. What questions?"

"Where did you find me?"

"You were lying unconscious just outside the barracks when I came running out after the storm."

"Why did you hide me?"

"I recognized you because of your hair."

She wasn't expecting this reply. "Why would you know anything about my hair?"

"Because your sister had the same hair."

"Sister? Which one?"

He shuffled his feet. "I don't know her name, but two red-haired girls came in about a month ago. The Warden made a big deal of it back then, made us all clean the entire camp because the Frost Queen was sending in some of her personal guards to test and collect these two."

"So you saw them come in?"

"Yeah, I was performing door duty that day. I remember the look in their eyes. They were very scared. I felt bad, but what can you do? There aren't many of us who are sympathetic to the prisoners. Most of the guards are brainwashed pretty well by the Warden, but a few of us help out where we can."

"By hiding us? What is the plan now?"

Ynya heard Thore swallow. "Hurry up, we need to get you hidden again."

With that, he stepped away from the door.

Ynya's rage began to build, but instead of tamping it down,

she let it bubble to the surface. He was hiding something, but she didn't know what. As much as she appreciated his help, she didn't like being lied to, and right now, he was avoiding answering something. She didn't know what, she didn't know why, but she was going to find out.

Ynya took the bag of food and water skins from him without a word.

Before Thore put the footlocker back, however, he paused, lying on the ground and looking at her. "Look, I know you're scared and worried, but things are going to take time. After that storm, there are guards swarming everywhere, patrolling every inch of this place on a regular schedule. I can't take you anywhere but here right now. Maybe in a month, once they give up looking, I might be able to move you to a safer location, but right now, it's just too risky."

He slid the locker halfway, then said, "I'm sorry, Ynya. I will get you out, but you're going to have to be patient."

She was plunged into darkness once again.

Ynya sat there against the wall while Thore's bunkmates came in and the four chatted about the day's events. They prattled on about nothing for half an hour until another guard came by to tell them to get to sleep.

The rage she'd built up over their conversation never faded. It simmered, right below the surface.

She pulled out the knife she'd managed to grab off Thore's belt right as she crouched down to go into the wall.

It was incredibly sharp, a fact she verified by poking the top of her finger.

Chapter Twenty-Seven

❧❦❧

Despite being on her own, depending on someone bringing her food and water, Ynya wasn't entirely helpless.

She had a knife, and a purpose.

She also had the knowledge that the soldiers here moved to an extremely regimented schedule; a schedule she was going to exploit.

Ynya surmised that if the solder's time was this regimented, other parts of their lives were, too.

Her first step was to probe another wall opposite the spot where Thore's footlocker was located.

She waited until Thore and all his companions fell asleep, but before the soldiers on the other side came back.

Using the knife, she carved away at the back of the plaster, chipping it off a bit at a time. She was very careful not to raise the volume of her scraping above that of a mouse in the walls.

That's all I am, a secret mouse, who can't risk getting caught.

If fate needed her to be a mouse, she would be a mouse.

She made a single hole through the plaster, just big enough to poke the edge of the knife through.

Sure enough, after about half an inch through the air, the tip of the knife hit something wood and metal.

Footlocker.

Thank the God's Above and the Warden's insistence on being organized.

Ynya created three more holes, checking each carefully to ensure they were well-inside the area covered by the locker. After verifying the size, she severed the lines connecting each hole. Before she knew it, she had a cutout for a hole hanging on with just a few pieces of wood and plaster.

She had another exit from her prison.

Ynya ate while the second shift of soldiers bumped around inside the room and prepared for bed. She paid attention to the things they talked about, trying to glean any information she could from their conversation.

These particular soldiers were apparently rebuilding some walls in the Pit, and spent their day replanting posts and stretching fence line while another group of soldiers corralled the prisoners to a small section of the Pit.

The last part made Ynya hopeful. If all the prisoners were confined to a certain section of the Pit, that must mean there was extensive damage done to the structure. Extensive damage meant she would have a much easier time escaping through holes in fences.

She hoped that if everyone was so focused on rebuilding, then they wouldn't be focused on torturing.

It also meant she couldn't waste so much time anymore, because at the rate they repaired the compound, she wouldn't have much time to escape.

Escape.

The word was almost foreign to her, even though she'd only been in Reyoarfjell for a few days.

At least she hoped it had only been a few days.

The Warden's unique Enlightenment sessions had done a good job of preventing her from keeping track of the passage of time.

No time.

Ynya pursed her lips and furrowed her brow. That bastard had enjoyed toying with her. It was time for a payback. She would enjoy getting her magic back and giving him a lesson in how to cause pain.

If I get my magic back. It had been so long since she had it that she was beginning to wonder how it would be to have the power coursing through her chest once again. It terrified her to think that she was starting to get used to not having her heat anymore.

What is happening to me?

Ynya napped once the second shift soldiers went to sleep, mostly because she didn't want to risk scraping plaster and cutting wood while a soldier slept inches away. It was too risky. She might have one shot at escaping. She couldn't make a single mistake.

Shortly after the solders woke and prepared for their day, Ynya took the opportunity to do some exploration.

Given the patrol's thirty-minute schedule, she gave herself twenty minutes to look through as many rooms as she could.

Ynya pushed the footlocker away from the wall. She winced with every scrape against the stone floor.

Once it was pushed far enough, she shimmied out, listening every few seconds for the tell-tale sound of feet.

She repeated the action to move the footlocker back in

front of the hole. She would hate for anyone to come around the corner and see the locker out, then discover the hole.

Once they knew people were hiding, all the walls in the entire barracks would come down. Ynya didn't doubt for a second that the Warden would tear down his own soldier's homes in order to find missing prisoners. He would make everyone in his employ sleep in the cold if it meant she was found.

Ynya knew the risk she took, but she couldn't sit around all day doing nothing. She needed to move, she needed to feel like she was getting closer to finding her sisters and escaping.

She rummaged around in nine footlockers before hearing the methodical steps of the sentry.

Right on time.

Rather than run back to the safety of her wall, she climbed inside one of the lockers and waited. It was a little cramped, but she was small enough that it was an easy hiding place.

The soldier did his duty as expected. After a few dozen footsteps, pauses at each doorway, and a small sneezing fit, the soldier marched to the next hallway.

Thore's wing housed six rooms, with four soldiers per room. Ynya peeked her head out of the wing to find a long, spacious hallway running the length of whichever barracks she was in.

She stood in roughly the middle of the barracks, with three wings splitting off to one side, most likely the north, and four toward the south.

Given the stone floor below her, she surmised that she had to be on the ground floor. She had heard the clomp of the roaming soldier's boots above her, so there had to be a second floor.

Ynya reviewed the overall layout of the camp in her mind. The soldier barracks were on the east side of the camp, meaning this building was probably the building she'd first seen to the east when she and Synol had come into the camp at the southern entrance.

That meant this building was close to an exit. The two stories meant it was also close to the height of the fence that ran along the outside perimeter.

If she could figure out how to get to the second story, she might find a way to escape over the rooftop. Or at least a way to open the door from the wall.

Finally, she had enough information to begin and formulate a plan. She had a purpose, and she had a few hours until the prisoners came back. As long as she avoided the roaming sentry, she should be alone.

This meant supplies.

Every soldier stored something unique in their lockers in addition to the standard extra uniform, bedding, and marching pack. Ynya was especially delighted to find extra pieces of uniforms. One footlocker had an extra right boot, and two rooms over she found a matching left boot.

Another had the blue top, and the locker right next to that one held an extra set of blue pants. Only they were way too big for her, so she left those and kept rummaging.

Before long, she had collected enough pieces to give herself one cobbled-together uniform that actually fit. She thought about just taking an entire uniform, but one whole uniform missing would cause an inquiry. A handful of random pieces missing would be harder to pin down, especially if they were scattered across the entire floor of the barracks.

Shortly after the next guard pass, she went back to Thore's room and deposited her new uniform in the wall, along with some more items she'd found in the various lockers: two bottles of vodka, a shuttered lantern, a pack of matches, a hammer, a pair of snips, and her most precious items: three extra wool blankets.

Without her magic, she'd been so cold this whole time, and while she'd acclimated a tiny bit, her body still ached for the heat. It made sleeping, especially quietly, a difficult thing to do.

It had been just one more issue to deal with during the time she'd spent with the Warden, but now that she was out from under his thumb and had some time to take things she needed, she wanted to be warm.

Besides, she never knew how long she and her sisters would need to run from this place, and blankets seemed like a smart thing to take with them.

Especially if I never get my magic back.

She hung out near the entrance to this particular wing and watched the guard perform his rounds up and down the long hallway through the main barracks building.

Two minutes per wing, come out to the hallway, turn right, march to the next wing, turn right into the wing. Two minutes later, come out.

She followed behind him for an entire cycle, watching as he continued his right-hand turns and eventually hit a set of stairs in the center of the building.

So there is a way to the second floor.

The difficulty would be getting behind him so make sure she wasn't seen when she went upstairs.

For now, she needed to sleep.

After holing herself up in the wall once again behind Thore's lockbox, Ynya checked the second exit into the other barracks room to ensure it opened freely, that she could quietly set the extra piece of wall inside, and there was no evidence on the outside. She also made sure she could easily move the foot-locker from inside the wall.

Once she was sure that she had two exits out of her hiding spot, she curled up in her three blankets, and fell asleep.

Chapter Twenty-Eight

"Ynya?"

"Thore." Ynya peered through the opening and looked out at Thore.

"Come, we don't have a lot of time."

"I went to the bathroom earlier, while all the soldiers were away."

"You what?" The worry in his voice was palpable. "You shouldn't be taking risks like that."

"Thore, listen. I appreciate everything you've done for me, but I can't wait weeks for a chance to escape. My sisters are being tortured while I wait here. I don't even know what is going on with them."

He sighed. "If it's any consolation, all Enlightenments have stopped while the repairs are going on. I've seen your sister out in the Pit for the last two days."

"You waited two days to tell me this?"

Anger flashed to the surface, making Ynya's skin prickle at his admission. She was glad that she hadn't left the confines of her mid-wall hideout, because she would be afraid of what she might do with her knife if she were face-to-face with him. As it was, she had to fight the urge to scratch son of a bitch's face.

He swallowed. "I'm—I'm sorry for not telling you. I didn't want you to do anything rash."

She gritted her teeth. "That's not your decision to make."

His face hardened.

"It is, because I risked everything to save you. I could have left you unconscious on the side of the building. You would have been picked up by the next soldier a minute or two later. I did what I had to do at the time."

Ynya growled. "Well it doesn't seem to be helping much. Hiding people in walls for weeks on end while others die out there? How is that helping? Hiding one to kill a hundred?"

She knew she was overreacting, but she just couldn't help it. Days of pent-up anger and she had no way to release it.

Thore's eyes grew tight. "What would you have me do? Would you rather me not help anyone? I can only do so much within the bounds I have placed around me."

His voice lowered to a whisper, but had an edge she hadn't heard from him before. "If I don't help, who else will? I'd rather help one person than none. If you don't think that is enough, then I'm sorry. It's all I can do. I want to help you, I really do, but if you are going to put my life in jeopardy then I cannot go any further."

His hand flexed on the glow orb. "I've seen it happen in the past. A guard feels bad for the prisoners and helps them out, but doesn't enforce strict rules to keep them both safe. When they are discovered, all of us guards suffer for it. We are all put back into Enlightenment training to correct any aberrant thoughts.

"Any soldier found helping prisoners is killed, they don't trust the Enlightenment process again. Now the prisoners have lost one more person fighting for their lives. There aren't many of us left, and if we are found out, there is a chance that they will torture us for the rest of them. Is that a responsibility you want on your shoulders?"

Thore sighed, his face exhausted. "We used all our time arguing. They're going to be here soon. I beg you, please don't do anything rash yet, I will scout and find more information about your sister and I will do what I can to help you get to her, but I have to do it on my timetable."

He winced, waiting for her response.

Ynya pursed her lips. "I will be careful, that is all I can promise."

Thore nodded, clearly not happy with her reply, but also not wanting to argue further anymore. He pushed the foot-locker into place.

Ynya immediately took the opportunity to change into her stolen soldier outfit. After tucking her bright red hair into the hood they all wore, she carefully pushed the other footlocker away from the wall.

You can't tell me what to do.

Knife in hand, she snuck over to the other side of the room, pulled back the footlocker there, and began carving away at the wall.

Fifteen minutes later, and with plenty of time to clean up and hide inside the next wall over, Ynya climbed into the hidden alcove between the next bay of barracks.

This one was set up slightly different, because it ran into the staircase that led to the next floor.

Before sealing herself into this hidden alcove, she took a minute to look behind her at the footlocker that led to her original hiding spot.

Thore would be pissed, and if she was discovered, he

would be killed or punished. But she couldn't worry about that right now. She had to find her sisters and get them out of here.

She would do everything she could to keep Thore out of it, but her family came first.

Her sisters had to come first because they were all she had.

The staircase, it turned out, didn't have a full double-wall around it like the rest of the barracks rooms did. It was a curious design choice, but after a little poking around, she realized why.

The barracks had originally been a single floor, and one of the rooms had been converted to a staircase. In order to account for enough support for the new staircase, the walls had been taken out and thick posts had gone in their place.

So while she could see the second floor between the two large posts, the space between was much smaller than it had been before. It was so small, that even she might not be able to fit through there.

God's Below, this isn't going to be easy.

Ynya looked up between the thin walls again. If some of the plaster that squished between the lathe was knocked away, and if she supported herself on the large posts to the side, she might be able to fit her tiny frame through that opening. Even then she would probably need someone to help push her up.

Oh wait, there should be space under the stairs!

She had completely forgotten about the back part of the stairs. She was near the front, where the upstairs met the downstairs hallway.

Ynya worked her way through the wall to the other side of the barracks room to take a look at the back of the stairs. If the back side of the stairs were hollow, it meant she would be able to have more room to hide her sisters before they could escape.

She silently squeezed her way around the wall, and saw the larger opening under the stairs around the corner.

Something nagged at the back of her mind as she worked sideways through the wall, but she wasn't able to pinpoint what the concern was.

Ynya paused for a moment, listening intently through the wall. Nothing other than the breathing of soldiers behind her.

Ynya still couldn't figure out what bugged her, but as she continued sideways through the wall, she realized what the problem was.

Someone waited under the stairs, and as she came around the corner, she saw who.

Chapter Twenty-Nine

Ynya didn't move or breathe.

Two sets of eyes stared back at her.

For a long time, no one moved. No one said anything.

She looked between the two sets of eyes, trying to decipher what was going on. Her mind screamed at her to run.

Or hit something.

She held her mind's automatic reactions at bay, and allowed her eyes to take in the scene before her.

One girl, and one boy.

It took a second, but she recognized them.

A broad smile spread across her face as she realized who it was.

"Tyrain...and you must be Gustave's sister?"

It took a few pounding heartbeats for realization to bloom on Tyrain's face.

Ynya's heart sank as she watched him. He must have been terrified, listening to her climbing around in the wall without knowing what was about to come around that corner.

She also realized she still wore the soldier's uniform. That had to have made his worry that much worse as he saw the tell-tale blue of the uniform come around the corner.

It was a good thing neither of them screamed, or they would all be captured by now.

Ynya removed her hood to expose her chaotic red hair, then knelt down and extended her arm.

Gustave's sister cringed, but Tyrain took Ynya's hand.

"It's okay, Aelin, this is Ynya. She's a friend."

Ynya had only seen this girl from afar one time. She was pretty. Her hair was wild and unkempt, giving her even more of a chaotic look. She was about Synol's age, but the look in her eyes was like that of a frightened child, alert and scared.

Ynya embraced Tyrain.

"I'm so glad to know that you are alive. I heard that there were four prisoners missing. Do you know who the other one is?"

He shook his head. "I don't know, sorry. When the storm came, Gustave grabbed me and his sister and shoved us into the clocktower just as the storm hit with full-force. We huddled inside for a long time until the worst of it was over, then he scouted outside. Most of the fence on this side of the Pit was down, so he put her hand in mine, told her I was a friend, told us both to run."

Ynya smiled at Aelin.

"Hi Aelin, my name is Ynya. I'm a friend of Tyrain. I also know your brother Gustave. Your brother is a smart and strong man."

Ynya watched the recognition in Aelin's eyes as her brother was mentioned, but she didn't reply.

"How did you get here?" Tyrain asked.

Ynya filled him in on her story thus-far. "I have some food back in my cubby, have you eaten?"

He shook his head. "No, we ran around the outside of the barracks to try to find shelter and huddled under some broken debris back there. Aelin leaned against the wall and fell through though, and realized the bricks had only been stacked and led into this space." He pointed behind Ynya.

She turned, realizing she'd been so focused on the two figures on the ground she hadn't paid attention to her surroundings.

Just like she had thought, the space under the stairs was hollow, but for a thick post in the center to support the stairs above.

The entire back wall of the stairs was made of brick, possibly an older building material, for the outsides of the building.

Upon careful inspection, she realized some of the bricks were loose, enough that a small hole could be uncovered. It was barely big enough for a person to fit through, but that was enough to allow them to hide in here.

"Careful. It took me a while to arrange them like that and I know there are a lot of patrols that go back there regularly. We don't want them to see."

Ynya turned back to her terrified friends.

"Let me go back to my hiding spot and get you some food. Everyone should be asleep so if I'm very slow and careful, I should be able to get back soon."

It took her longer than she expected. She'd only snuck around like this when there were no soldiers present. Four snoring soldiers in their bunks was a much scarier proposition than none.

Ynya waited three minutes after the sentry had passed, then made her move.

She couldn't make a mistake. It wasn't just her life on the line, or Thore's anymore.

But now I have a way to exit the barracks through the back!

Half an hour later, she returned with most of the items she had taken from the rooms earlier that day.

She ate half a roll of bread for herself, and gave the rest of the rations to the others.

"I'm going to have to go leave and scout around. It's the middle of the night right now, so if I'm going to be able to do any walking around in this uniform and not get noticed, now is my best chance."

Tyrain nodded.

"Have you heard or seen Joanne?"

He shook his head. "Sorry, when the storm hit it was pure chaos, I was lucky to be by Gustave when I did. A lot of the Pit was damaged, and a bunch of the prisoners immediately ran for the breaks in the fences. For the first day I heard the shouts of the prisoners as they were found and dragged back to the Pit. We're lucky we didn't get discovered because one of them was captured just on the other side of this wall hiding under the same piece of rubble we did. We listened to the whole thing as the soldiers yelled, asking if they knew where anyone else was."

Ynya shivered. "So they found everyone but us three and one more?"

He shrugged. "I'm not sure, sorry."

"Well, I better get out there and see what I can do. You two stay here, and stay quiet. I'll be back as soon as I can, before the sun comes up.

With that, she moved the small pile of bricks, worked herself through the wall, and out into the open air of Reyoarfjell.

Chapter Thirty

It was both exhilarating and terrifying being out under the stark night sky.

Ynya paused to breathe in the air. It felt so cold in her lungs, but it was one step closer to freedom.

After replacing the bricks and arranging some of the rubble to hide it even better, she took her first steps into the terrifying world. She tried to remember how the sentries walked. It was slow, methodical, and in time to some inner clock. Ynya made it to end of the barracks and peeked around.

Two long breaths later, she told herself what she was going to do.

Go out, make a loop around, and come back. Make sure you look like you belong, and you will not rouse any suspicions. You are a soldier in the Frost Queen's army, act like it.

She didn't believe herself, but she took the first step. She took a second, then a third. Soon, she marched in a clockwise direction around Reyoarfjell.

There was still a lot of extensive damage. The gate leading

out to the east lay on its side partially blocking the large doorway to freedom. The southern one was completely gone, along with half of the wall. Three towers-worth of rubble lay along the outer wall, and the bell tower that normally stood at the north-west corner of the Pit had the top ripped off. The double fences that separated the Pit from the rest of the camp had been almost entirely destroyed. At least half of the various buildings around the camp were missing large chunks of their roof.

It was the dead of night and the entire place was a ghost-land. A few sentries roamed, half-heartedly making their rounds, and half a dozen guards stood at corners and cross-roads, struggling to keep their eyes open.

It was the perfect time for her to be out here.

She slowed her gait to match the sleepy nature of the overnight shift. She didn't want to stand out by keeping perfect time with her movements. Worst of all, she didn't want any of them to talk to her.

As she marched around, she took note of the Pit.

Temporary walls were erected around the south-western part of the Pit, closest to the prisoner barracks. At least two hundred prisoners huddled together in the cold dark night.

Most of the prisoner barracks had been leveled. Over half of it was demolished in a pile, and the roof had been ripped off the rest.

Wow, Finny, you are one powerful girl.

It was a bit terrifying, how intense her sisters were when they unleashed their magic. Ynya was able to heat things up, set a few things on fire, but ultimately she could only affect things she could touch.

That was nothing compared the destruction Synol did when she buried an entire camp of soldiers.

And that was nothing, still, compared to the terrifying winds Finny conjured.

A chill ran up Ynya's spine at the memory of that night. She couldn't shake the dead-eyed stare her sister gave when they last looked at each other.

That hadn't been Finny controlling that cyclone. That had been someone else.

Or something else.

What did they do to you, Finny?

Ynya didn't want to know.

As Ynya approached the far side of the Pit, where all the prisoners huddled, she tried to make out her sister's red hair. Half a dozen prisoners saw her walking past and pled with her to give them more food, water, or blankets.

She wanted to go to them and give them everything she could, but she was alone out here in a stolen guard's uniform. She had nothing on her to give. Ynya forced her gaze from the prisoners and looked forward, hiding her shame.

As she walked, the prisoners' pleas continued. Their cries roused a handful of guards on the wall and at their posts who straightened up. One yelled back at the prisoners to be quiet.

With each step, Ynya remembered her earlier conversation with Thore. She told him that she would do whatever it took to get her sister back. But now, walking past all these prisoners, in the dead of night, she couldn't even bring herself to look at them.

She realized now what a knife's edge he walked.

If she pulled down her hood and exposed herself to those prisoners, their shouts, even of joy, would bring the guards. They would capture and torture her once again.

The would find Tyrain and Aelin.

And she didn't want to think about what they would do to Synol. Or Finny.

I'm sorry, Thore. I get it now.

Ynya made two more rounds throughout the entire encampment, each circuit taking her about half an hour. She spent the next two after that paying attention to the guards. She noted where they all patrolled, and which ones slept at their posts.

Then, she saw him.

Gustave.

He stood in the soldier's barracks while he donned a coat. Even from halfway across the camp, she recognized his bulky frame and his casual nature.

As soon as she saw him, she wanted to shout and wave. Ynya tamped down the desire burning in her chest to greet him. She quickened her pace, however, because she wanted to make sure he knew his sister was safe.

He spoke a few words to the guard outside the barracks and walked toward the broken bell tower.

The bell tower?

If he was awake, that meant the shifts would soon start, which meant more soldiers.

She needed to talk to him before that happened.

She sped up even more, while sticking to a pace befitting a soldier on the job. She cut across where the Pit used to be, intersecting with him just as he arrived to the bell tower.

"Gustave." Her voice was hoarse and low, due to the over-whelming fear gripping her body as she approached him.

He looked up and she saw the terrified look in his eyes.

Chapter Thirty-One

Gustave's eyes widened to the size of cups, and he shook his head slowly.

To his left side, down by his leg, he spun his index finger in a circle, while his eyes gestured three times in the direction of his hand.

Is he telling me to take another lap around the camp?

Ynya nodded, then continued right past him. But she caught the slight hint of a smile.

What was that about?

Twenty paces away from him, she heard the one voice she hadn't wanted to hear. The one voice that would set all the nerve endings in her young body on edge.

"Gustave, I was wondering when you would join me. You are two minutes late, you know."

The Warden.

Her stomach lurched as she continued her march around the camp. She hadn't seen him at all! How could she have *not* noticed?

Turning the corner, she chanced a quick look back to see

the Warden deep in conversation with Gustave. They held a paper between the two of them, and Gustave nodded.

They must be going over today's schedule.

She swallowed, suddenly very parched. She'd come very close to getting caught. She shouldn't be so cavalier to announce her presence while walking through a crowd.

Worse yet was the notion that the Warden had been at the bell tower this whole time and she hadn't noticed him.

What if he had noticed me?

Ynya thought back to the first time she and the Warden crossed paths. He said that she and Synol stood out because they hadn't used the correct hand signals, thus alerting the soldiers to their presence.

What if all the lazy, sleepy soldiers had been watching her the whole time, knowing exactly who she was? What if they were waiting for her to head back divulge where the other prisoners hid?

The thought terrified Ynya more than anything, so much that her body shook uncontrollably. She struggled to put one foot in front of the other.

Focus, Ynya. Focus like your mother taught you.

She had to maintain her ruse a bit longer, then she could go back to the relative safety of the barracks.

Ynya focused. She pushed out all the negative thoughts and drew her mind into a point. She focused on her feet. One in front of the other. She focused on her breathing. One deep breath. Two deep breaths.

Ynya marched. She was a soldier in the Frost Queen's army, and she acted like one.

Her paced slowed once again. She needed time to think. She needed time to adjust to this new potential threat.

She passed by the place where she had been taken for her

Enlightenments. Ynya tensed as she walked by, not wanting to relive the memories of her torture the last time she was there. She increased her pace a bit.

As she walked by a thought popped into her head.

No wonder I can't find Synol in the crowd. She must still be in one of the Enlightenment rooms.

Instead of allowing her mind to reel down the path of despair and worry, she used the opportunity to study the prisoners in the Pit again. Ynya scanned over the crowd. There was no red hair, no Joanne, and no one else she recognized.

Another guard walked her direction, pulling the cries for help from the prisoners.

She tensed, just wanting to make it past the guard unseen, but a thought refused to leave her conscious.

Hand signals.

If the solders did use subtle hand signals to communicate with each other, then she would be noticed, if she hadn't been already.

As the approaching patrol passed by another one of the sleepy guards, she noticed the slight movement of his right hand. It was fast and performed right at the apex of his arm swing. He moved his thumb twice across the inside of his middle and index finger, like he was flicking away something from his thumbnail.

You sneaky bastards.

It was brilliant. Most people wouldn't even notice it given the cupping of the hand hiding the thumb. Even if they did, many would think it simply a random hand tic. The sleepy guard didn't do anything different, so the approaching roaming guard performed it once again.

This time, the sleepy standing guard must have noticed the

movement because he pursed his lips and replied with his left hand using the same motion.

Seemingly satisfied, the patrolling guard continued.

He passed by one more, but didn't use the signal.

They must not be using it every time.

Maybe it was more of a spot check to ensure that each soldier was awake and paying attention once or twice a shift, but came in handy as a means to identify anyone who didn't belong.

That must mean that they began using it after someone else broke into here.

The idea excited Ynya. At some point, someone else had broken into Reyoarfjell and had disrupted things so much that the army had to implement new procedures to rout out any infiltrators.

It was her turn, as the patrolling soldier turned in her direction.

They locked eyes for a moment, before she got her gaze squarely on the ground in front of her.

One foot in front of the other, Ynya.

He did the hand signal.

She raised her right hand–

Wrong hand!

She took two more steps.

He performed his hand movement once again. His left hand tensed as it slowly went for the dagger on his belt.

She replied with the same motion from her left, and she kept on moving, one foot in front of the other.

His left hand relaxed and he continued walking past her.

As much as she wanted, Ynya didn't turn around. She didn't want to make any more mistakes this morning.

Chapter Thirty-Two

Ynya rounded the corner of the Pit. In the distance, she saw the first hints of the early-morning sun peek over the mountain tops.

The bells chimed, signifying wake up time for the first shift.

Shit!

She'd been out too long. *If I head back now I'll be found out!*

Or maybe it was the perfect distraction.

With a few dozen guards waking up and beginning manual labor, it might be the perfect time for her to talk to Gustave, since he wouldn't chime the bells for another hour. She slowed her approach, surveying the area around the bell tower carefully.

Rubble from the destroyed tower had been cleared away to reveal the three bells. The smaller one had a crack in it but still rang, as it had been re-hung on a wooden post along with its companions. The larger of the three had a huge chunk in the debris a few feet away. They were damaged, but functional.

Most importantly, no Warden.

She checked and double-checked the shadows just inside the doorway of the now decrepit tower.

Can I trust my own eyes when I'd walked past the exact spot at least twice before without seeing him?

Gustave finished his bell ringing and put away his mallets.

It was now or never. She would go in carefully and test before announcing who she was to him.

Ynya glanced at his ordinals as he put away the mallets.

"1811." She tried to keep her voice as deep and as commanding as possible.

He looked up, a concerned expression on his face.

The expression melted away when their eyes met.

Gustave glanced around before nodding his head toward the side. He stepped behind the broken tower and grabbed some rubble from the ground with massive hands.

Ynya approached him, happy to see a friendly face.

"Stay there," he warned. His voice was low and strained.

She halted, realization hitting her. It would probably look very bad if a soldier hugged one of the prisoners. She needed to remember her role.

He moved another piece of rubble. "Glad to see you."

"Likewise. I saw your sister and Tyrain. They are safe."

He paused, mid-throw, emotion palpable on his strained face. "I'm glad to hear that."

She glanced around. A couple groggy soldiers took their first steps from the front door of the barracks.

"Have you seen Synol? I didn't see her in the Pit."

He cocked his chin toward the north. "The Warden moved her from the Pit to the Enlightenment area recently."

Ynya tensed, deep-seated worry knotting the muscles in

her back. The thought of Synol being alone with that man sickened her to her core.

Her next words were strained, angry, said through gritted teeth. "Which door?"

He frowned. "Second from the left, I believe, but she could be anywhere in that building and it will be swarming with his men."

She knew where one of her sisters was, at least.

Ynya glanced back at the soldiers coming out of the barracks. She didn't have much time as they headed this direction to begin their day of hauling away rubble.

Ynya needed to think. She needed space and time. She didn't have either of those right now.

If she didn't go back to Tyrain and Aelin, they would have no food for today.

A thought caused her to freeze.

If Thore doesn't find me there when he wakes for his shift, what will he do? Turn himself in in the hopes that he gets a lesser punishment?

Ynya had less than an hour to get back into that wall. If she headed back now, she could sneak into the room next to Thore's and be there with plenty of time. She would also be able to grab the supplies she'd left there.

Maybe he would turn me in?

All he had to do was report the discovery of a network of tunnels leading through the barracks. All he had to say was that he noticed something odd this morning when he went to open his footlocker and the Warden would turn the place inside out to find her.

With her expanded path, it would look like he was just a hapless bystander who happened to be next to one of the walls that she'd carved out of. She'd even stolen his knife, which would be even more evidence that she had orchestrated the whole thing. They would find and capture Tyrain and Aelin. They would torture them for information on her.

I'd be found sooner rather than later.

If she tried to save Synol right now, she'd be doing it when all the soldiers were up and awake, probably the worst time for her to attempt a rescue.

Besides, the Warden was probably with Synol right now.

That thought sickened her more than anything. It made her want to run toward the Enlightenment rooms and tear the place down.

Damn! I need my magic back!

"Do you know where Finny is?"

Gustave shot her a confused look.

"My younger sister. She's why we even came here. She's the one who caused the storm."

His eyes widened.

Ynya continued, lowering her voice even more. "I think they're doing the same things to her that they did to your sister. I saw her the night of the storm. Her eyes were...not hers."

Realization warmed over his face and he nodded. "If she caused the storm, then she's probably in with the Translator, to the south." He cocked his head toward the white building directly across from them. "But it wouldn't be the same thing that they did to my sister. The Translator does...other things to them. He experiments on them, trying to create a new breed of soldiers for the Frost Queen."

The Translator?

Finny and Synol were on opposite sides of the compound. *Which do I choose?*

Ynya looked back at the barracks. If she left right now, it would appear that she was just coming in from her overnight shift. No one would be the wiser, and she, dressed in her soldier uniform, would have full run of the place. She'd be able to gather additional weapons, something she would need if she didn't have her magic.

The vodka would come in handy, too. Fire was always useful, and it might be a good substitute for her lack of magic.

Synol was with the evilest man she'd ever met, and Finny's mind was being tortured out of her. Ynya couldn't bear the thought that Finny could turn out like Aelin.

In her mind, something clicked into place.

It wasn't a plan, but more of an urging. It was a need she couldn't ignore any longer.

Ynya didn't know what she was going to do, she didn't know how she was going to do it, but her mind made the decision for her, and waited for the rest of her to catch up.

She took two steps closer and lowered her voice even more as she spoke into Gustave's ear.

"Your sister is under the stairs in the barracks. They have a few weapons, and thick blankets to help survive the wilds. I'm going to go get my sisters and make a run for it."

She didn't wait for his reply.

Ynya Oblique turned for the Enlightenment rooms and marched north toward them to save her sister.

She would always run toward family.

Chapter Thirty-Three

2201's world was nothing but pain.

Her bones had been broken and healed so many times she had lost count.

Above her, the Translator continued his lesson as he held up the final vial of serum.

"We're making good progress, and her mind has held on reasonably well. Only one more serum to go. This last one will unleash the final changes, and seal all the changes we've done into one cohesive unit."

He addressed another soldier who replaced his lost assistants. The new assistant always looked at her in horror.

The Translator looked at her with a childish delight.

"I know the serums are making some...erratic modifications to her body structure, but once they take, I hope you will see the artistry that has been so many years coming."

The terrified assistant glanced down at her wrists and ankles, noting 2201's restraints for the fourth time since she had entered the room.

<<*He's changing you into a monster.*>> The voice came

back the second day in, the fourth time her bones broke and grew heavier.

I'm doing it for the glory of the Frost Queen.

<<*The Frost Queen doesn't know he's doing this to you. She wanted you for herself. He stole you from her.*>>

The Translator continued. "As you can see, the elongated jaw and extra row of teeth are a curious adaptation, but I think Her Majesty will find a use for her, don't you think?"

<<*You are already a monster, he's just changing your body match your soul*>> the voice said.

"But we can't celebrate quite yet. While the same changes occurred with the last patient, his mind was too far gone to be of any use."

The assistant stammered. "Is that the thing we shipped out a week ago?"

The Translator stood up from examining 2201. He smiled. "Yes, it was, in fact. What did you think about my creation?"

The assistant looked between 2201 and the doctor with the syringe of brown liquid in his hands. "Terrifying."

The Translator turned back to 2201, leaning over her arm and plunging the final syringe into her arm.

"Then I succeeded."

Chapter Thirty-Four

Ynya marched up to the second door from the left in the Enlightenment building. She made the motion with her hand, hoping the soldier next to the door would take her for a superior.

He returned the motion, even bowing slightly and opening the door for her.

Her nerves were shot as she went through the door. She didn't know what to expect.

Inside was a small room, like one she'd encountered when she and Synol looked for the records.

Left, right, or center?

Ynya chose center.

She opened the door and was shocked to see a familiar face as she walked through.

Joanne, with a woman huddled over her left shoulder.

The Inscriber.

White hot rage filled Ynya's vision as the memory of all the pain that woman had caused her filled her mind.

The Inscriber turned. "What is it? I'm almost done—"

She didn't finish her sentence, because Ynya shoved her knife into the woman's throat.

Blood spurted from the woman's opened neck, spraying Joanne, who looked on with a mixture of horror and confusion.

"Joanne, I'm so glad to see you."

Joanne looked at the Inscriber's body as it slumped to the ground, a wild and shocked look in her eyes.

"It's alright, I'm here, Joanne. I know they've been torturing you for a while now. I know where Tyrain is. Are you well?"

Joanne's wide eyes took a moment to process everything, but they slowly came to focus on Ynya's face.

"Ynya?"

Ynya pulled her hood back, exposing her wild red hair. "I'm here for you Joanne. She won't hurt you anymore. Do you know where Synol is?"

Joanne shook her head. "I heard her screams, but I haven't in a while." Her face was white as snow, a stark contrast to the bright red blood splattered on her torso and chin.

Ynya helped her friend stand. "Come, I'm getting you out of here, but we have to find Synol."

Joanne nodded, still a little delirious.

Ynya felt bad for her sudden attack. *No one should have to be party to that sort of violent death, but I couldn't risk the Inscriber alerting anyone.*

They were all short on time here. They needed to hurry.

Joanne was wobbly, but she stood on her own. "You said you know where Tyrain is?"

Ynya nodded. "Yes, behind the barracks there are some loose bricks. You can find him there." She wiped the blade on the woman's shirt, cleaning off most of the blood. "We need to find you a soldier's uniform. It's our best chance at getting across the prison and getting to everyone. Once we get out of here, I don't know what is going to happen."

Joanne nodded. She couldn't stop staring at the dead woman on the floor.

After putting her hood back up to hide her hair, Ynya grabbed Joanne's hand. "Come, let's find Synol and we'll figure out what to do after that."

Ynya peeked her head back out of the first room.

Still clear.

She decided to go right this time.

It led to a small hallway with four doors along the back wall.

Ynya paused outside the doorway and listened.

First door was silent.

She debated opening it to peek in, but thought it best to check all the rooms just in case.

"Wait here," she whispered to Joanne, "I'm going to check each room for sound first."

Joanne nodded, taking a step back through the doorway into the front room.

Ynya crept along the hallway, pausing at each doorway, listening.

Outside the third, she heard the tell-tale sounds of soft crying.

Synol.

She would recognize that voice anywhere.

A quick glance back to Joanne, who watched her from the doorway, and Ynya moved to the fourth door. She wanted to make sure all rooms were empty before barging in to free Synol.

No sound.

Ynya only had one room to deal with.

She nodded to Joanne with a smile, then slowly opened the door.

Ynya stopped just as she entered in.

It was the same wooden room she'd been in with the Warden.

Synol sat in the same wooden chair. Leather straps around her wrists and ankles pinned her to the chair.

No one else was in the room.

"Ynya?" Synol's eyes lit up for a second as she recognized her sister.

"Syni."

Ynya was across the room and embracing her sister in a heartbeat. "I'm here, Synol. I'm here and I'm never going to leave you again."

Ynya worked at the straps to undo Synol from the chair. "Where are all the guards? I expected you to be monitored more than you were."

"I only had the one. She left me a few minutes ago when the Inscriber came for her."

"What did they do to you? Are you okay?"

Synol stared out the doorway, not looking at Ynya. "At first, when they took you and I both away, they tried to break me, but I resisted."

Synol grit her teeth as she stared out the door. "Ever since the storm hit, he's been playing mind games with me, telling me that he's torturing you."

She looked up at Ynya, a tear streaking down her face.

"I thought he was out torturing you when I didn't give the right answers to his questions, or when I didn't play his stupid games."

Ynya cupped Synol's face, her heart breaking. "I escaped during the storm that Finny created."

"Finny?"

Synol's lower lip trembled, and her face scrunched up at the name.

Ynya fought to keep her composure. Simply saying the name was enough to send her over the edge, but she needed to keep her mind focused. She worked on the next strap.

"Finny is here. She's the one who caused the storm with her magic. They have her to the south."

Synol let out an audible sob, and Ynya paused to embrace her sister. "I know. We are going to get her after this, I just need to find you and Joanne a soldier's uniform."

"Joanne?"

"Yeah," Ynya turned to indicate the hallway. "I found her in the first room getting more ordinals inscribed. She's waiting for us out there." Ynya popped off the last hand strap and knelt down to work on the third.

"Ynya." Synol's voice had a new edge. Love and anguish had been replaced by genuine terror.

"What?"

"Joanne is my guard. She's one of them."

Chapter Thirty-Five

Ynya barely registered the motion, but she felt it.

Joanne tackled her from behind, throwing her away from Synol.

Ynya's head hit the wall, followed by her shoulder. Pain shot up her arm from the blow.

Her eyes swam and filled with tears. She struggled to stay upright and turned to face her attacker.

In a heartbeat, the silver dagger stuck Ynya three times. She crumpled to the floor, a mass of bones and meat.

At least she didn't have to go through her magic disappearing again this time. It had already been gone so long she almost forgot what the burning heat in her chest felt like.

"And thus the elusive mage returns back to my den. I'm sorry I didn't have a buffet ready to receive you."

Joanne grabbed Ynya and yanked her to her feet, pinning her against the wall.

The Warden stood in the doorway, leaning casually against the jam. "I have to say, the colors look good on you. I can't wait to finish your training so that we can get you both into proper uniforms. Perhaps you can replace Kalda after killing her so unceremoniously. I think your red hair would look very good against the white outfit, don't you?"

Joanne tossed Ynya onto the wooden table.

Synol moved toward her sister but Joanne shoved her back into the chair. "Stay where you are."

The Warden loomed over Ynya. "I do need to thank you for telling us where the final two prisoners are. I'll send Joanne to go collect them shortly. But first, I think it's time we stop all the games and get down to why you're really here."

He put a gloved hand on Ynya's chin, turning her head back and forth while he inspected her.

"The Frost Queen needs more Skarmyord, and we've lost too many lately. Your little fight with one didn't help either, Ynya. I intend on replacing what you've taken from me." He turned to Synol. "Plus, siblings tend to all be about the same when it comes to the process, so that means I'll get myself two for the price of one."

He shoved Ynya's head to the side, forcing her to face the wall.

"Leave her alone!" Synol exclaimed. She grabbed the silver blade from Joanne's scabbard, and head-butted the surprised Skarmyord, knocking her over the table and into a heap on the ground.

Synol swung the blade at the Warden, causing him to jump back.

He laughed.

"Silly little girl, you think you can defeat me with a simple knife?"

He stepped back as Synol lunged again. "I'll show you how much fun it is!"

Joanne regained her composure and kicked, knocking the blade from Synol's grasp.

In a flash of silver, a dagger punctured Synol thrice again. She crumpled to a heap on the chair.

Only this time, it wasn't Joanne who did the stabbing, it was the Warden.

He flashed a grin while he pulled a handkerchief from a pocket and polished his blade. "You forget that I'm Skarmyord as well, dear girl. All that time spent with me and you never figured it out? You never made the connection?"

He sat down on the table next to Ynya. "You have to understand that you are not going to win here. You have no power, and every time you think you do, you are knocked back down into the gutter once again. There will be only one winner in the war that is coming, and you should feel lucky that I'm helping you find the winning side."

He stood, replacing the handkerchief, then frowned at Joanne.

In one swift motion, he backhanded her.

A sickening *crack* of bone filled the air. She flew backward and hit the wall, splintering the thick wood planks.

"Skarmyord are ready at any time to serve, they do not drop their blades, or misplace them." He took two steps over to her, and kicked downward with his heel.

Another sickening bone crack rang through the small room.

Ynya's stomach wrenched at the sound. It was a good thing she couldn't move, or she would be throwing up.

"And you NEVER allow someone to take your weapon from you!"

He turned, letting out a long, slow breath through his nostrils. "I'm sorry you girls had to witness that. I normally run a tight ship around here, but lately it seems that rules are being viewed as suggestions rather than critical to the health of the army. I think it's time that a new, stricter policy be enforced, and I think you three will be the perfect examples of what will happen if you do not obey. Every step of your change will be lauded for everyone in the camp to see. Two prisoners completing their Enlightenment and transition into Skarmyord, and one Skarmyord who will learn her place and understand how not to let your guard down."

He pulled his handkerchief out once more and coughed into it. "It's clear to me now, like it should have been. For too long, we've been lax with our regimen. That needs to end now.

"If we are going to get our little experiment prison back into shape, it all starts with discipline. It's time to expedite your training. How ever long it takes, regardless of how much pain I have to inflict on you, you both will be wielding blades soon, so I want you to prepare. We are just getting started here."

He turned, yelling out the door. "Guards! Take all three to the Translator. It's time we put them all straight through the Third Enlightenment."

Chapter Thirty-Six

☙❦☙

The fifth serum broke all her bones, even the ones she didn't know she had.

Her jaw elongated, adding teeth and bite strength.

Her elbows and knees broke and re-knit backward, like an animal's.

Long, terrifyingly sharp talons grew from her fingernails, tapering to a fine point.

Her torso expanded, giving her more muscles and strength. Strength to do the Frost Queen's bidding.

Her legs were longer now, with taut muscles for sprinting and jumping. The talons on her back legs were not as long as the ones on her front legs, but they were thicker. Better for digging.

Better for crushing bones if they needed.

Each time she metamorphosed, the incredible agony washed over her once again. She couldn't remember a time when she did not hurt. The torment was so intense, she begged for it to stop, even for a moment. Just a moment of rest is all she wanted from the overwhelming torment raging inside her body.

He stood over her, watching, waiting.

Every time she begged, he frowned.

He would not stop the pain.

He formed her into something greater, something the world had never seen. She had to endure the pain. She would be his greatest creation.

She begged for just a moment once again. Just one second to breathe fully. Her chest ached so much. She didn't think that she couldn't handle the pressure any longer.

His face scrunched and got red. He was angry.

"If you aren't strong enough to handle it, then you will disappoint not only me, but the Frost Queen. I will not stop this for you or anyone else. I would rather see your mind and body break than give up now.

"The pain will never go away. You were born in it, raised in it. You're formed into a creature of pain, and you will never forget it. If I let off now, even for a second, you will remember your old life, and I cannot do that. Even a moment of reprieve, might give you enough hope to give up. I refuse to fail!

"Her Majesty will never forgive me if I gave her anything less than perfect. Give in. Give in to the serum. Feel it fill your body with strength, with ferocity, and malice. Love the pain, for your world will be consumed by it. You will never leave it."

She knew he was right. When she finished her transformation, she would live with pain every day.

He turned to address his new assistant. "I must leave. Watch her and keep the straps tight."

Despite his command, the assistant stood by the door, shaking. Her eyes never left 2201.

The assistant understood. The assistant would leave too.

<<I never left you.>>

It was the voice.

The voice never left her.

The voice sung to her in her darkest times.

The voice cried alongside her with every bone snap, with every severed artery that had to be mended.

<<I'm sorry they did this to you. I'm sorry I wasn't able to help. I'm sorry that I wasn't able to communicate with my sister properly. I'm sure she wanted to help us, but she's captured now and won't be able to come rescue us.>>

2201 understood. 2201 had spent her entire life captured. She spent most of her time strapped to a table or chair.

<<If you are the most powerful thing in this room, why do they strap you down?>>

The Frost Queen needs me to help in her war.

<<What war?>>

The war to kill any that stand in Her way.

<<Like you?>>

I never stood in Her way.

<<Yes, you did. You once stood proud and tall, like my sister Ynya.>>

I know that name.

<<You know more than her name. You know her face. You saw her just a couple days ago, during the storm.>>

I saw a girl with red hair. She was the only one who didn't cower before me.

<<That was Ynya. She's not afraid of anything. She once fought a frost bear and won.>>

Nonsense!

<<It's true. You know it's true. She told you herself. She

showed you the tuft of fur from the bear. You used to have red hair like her.>>

Leave me be. I serve the Frost Queen. I never had red hair. I am claws and sinew. Still, she remembered Ynya showing her the tuft of fur when Mama wasn't looking.

<<You had the red hair, until the Translator made it all fall out. He took it from you, and replaced it with spines.>>

He did not. I have always been like this.

<<No, you were once a girl, but they took you from your mother and father. They stole you from your home town and brought you here. They tortured you and twisted you into the creature you are today. They took away your memories and family and bright red hair. They removed all of your freckles and made you into a monster that has to be strapped down to the table for them to be safe around you.>>

You don't know any of this.

<<Yes I do, because I used to be you. I am Finny. I am the little girl who used to run around with pig tails and bright red cheeks. I wore boy's clothes and refused to wear a dress except on God's day. That was me, and that was you. You did all those things, but now you allow them to do these things to you.>>

The Frost Queen needs me.

<<Your mother needed you. Your sisters needed you. Your father needed you. They all loved you, but the Frost Queen took you from them. For what? For pain? You heard the Translator. Your life will never stop being painful.>>

Leave me alone. I have a purpose. I will serve, and I will become great.

Finny was silent for a long while, so long that 2201 felt the pain creep back into her mind. Without Finny to talk to, she had nothing in her life but pain.

Finally, just as 2201 was beginning to think Finny was gone for good, after hours and hours of nothing but increasing pain as her bones broke and re-knit, Finny spoke once again.

<<*You already were great. You were better than great, you were happy.*>>

Chapter Thirty-Seven

✦❖✦

Ynya stopped trying to struggle against her bonds as they carried her past the Pit.

As one, the prisoners turned their heads, staring at the two sisters as the guards carted them south, toward the Translator.

It wasn't just the prisoners who stopped, the guards in the camp did as well.

Ynya remembered when she first entered the camp, when the door to the white building opened. She remembered prisoners and guards alike, stopping to pay respects to the limp bloody body as it was carted off, never to be seen again.

In that one singular moment, the entire camp came together as one.

Ynya now realized why it was so important. She recognized the look in everyone's faces.

The prisoners had lost one of their own, someone taken to the breaking point and beyond. A sister, a father, someone they huddled with under the cold unforgiving sky, was now dead.

Similarly, the guards had lost a recruit. Not all survived the treatments. Few endured the Third Enlightenment.

At that moment, the guards lost one more to their ranks. One more companion to chat with them along the wall. One more bunkmate, or mess hall conversation.

Every person, including the Warden, watched.

Including Thore.

He dropped the rocks he carried. His work long forgotten, he locked sorrowful eyes with her once again.

Thore narrowed his vision and pursed his lips, a downcast look on his dark face.

Ynya felt horrible for abandoning him, after all that he had done for her, but she couldn't stand by and not help her sister. He had to understand that.

Ynya realized that he would be discovered now. Her escape and admission to Joanne about the location of Tyrain and Aelin had sealed the fate of all the soldiers with tunnels behind their footlockers.

She wished she could tell Thore she was sorry. He stuck his neck out for her and she hadn't appreciated the gesture like she should have. There were any number of ways she could have handled the situation to keep him from being discovered, but once again, in her haste to find her sister, she caused harm to someone else through her actions.

She didn't know if it was fate, or dumb luck, but he was three steps from Gustave. His was another whose fate was probably sealed. Once they found Aelin with Tyrain, it would be all over for both of those men.

It was over for all of them.

Both men stood tall and somber as they watched their friends carried south, to the white buildings.

Ynya realized that both Gustave and Thore weren't looking at just her. In front of her was Joanne. They had both been Joanne's friend as well. Despite Joanne's conversion to Skarmyord, only a few days ago she had been a friend.

Ynya couldn't forgive her for her betrayal, but still felt awful for the way she had been tortured into becoming what she was now.

And yet, Joanne still wore prisoner clothes, while Ynya wore a guard's outfit. *What do the prisoners think about that? Do they care?*

Joanne's broken body led the group toward the white-roofed buildings near the southeastern exit to the prison. Her broken leg swung limp, probably causing incredible pain with each bounce. Yet she didn't make a sound, not a whimper.

Ynya glanced back to the men, wishing she could yell and warn them.

Please Gustave, please go save your sister and Tyrain. Go now, before the Warden comes for them.

Chapter Thirty-Eight

❦

"Take them through here and strap them in the other room. I will get to them soon. I have to monitor the speed of the serum as her final transformation takes hold."

The entire group paused in the doorway as they took in the sight of 2201.

More than one guard almost lost their stomachs at the sight. They all trembled as they gazed upon her form strapped to the table.

She smelled their fear from the across the room. It was a new sense she hadn't used until now. It was already proving useful.

The voice returned, crying out in exasperation at the three forms carried to the other room.

<<Ynya! Synol! My sisters! Where are they taking them?>>

The small sweet voice that spoke to 2201 filled with anguish.

Even though it wasn't physical pain, it was somehow worse than what 2201 endured.

She didn't know that there were other types of pain. She

hadn't known that someone else could feel pain like hers but in a different way.

They have your sisters?

<<*They have our sisters.*>> Finny sobbed. <<*We grew up with them. You know them. They are going to be turned into monsters for the Frost Queen.*>>

2201 watched as soldiers hauled the three girls into the other room.

The room where she'd seen the first creature.

She remembered his twisted features. She remembered his howls of anguish. She remembered the claw marks on the walls.

She remembered the soldiers replacing the glass.

They turned me into the same monster? Am I the same being that they had locked up in that room?

Finny didn't reply, but deep within the silence, 2201 felt the yearning. She wanted to see the girls again.

A memory popped into her mind. It was only a moment, a second, like the reprieve from pain she had asked of the Translator.

She remembered being a girl.

She had forgotten what it was like. She had forgotten what she used to be before all the pain and broken bones. She had been a girl before the claws and backwards legs.

I don't want to be that creature. I don't want to be twisted and hunched on all fours.

<<*You don't have to. You don't have to do anything you don't want to. Fight the serum. If you don't like what you've changed into, then take control. You can always change the parts of your life you don't like.*>>

∽

They strapped Ynya down, with Synol next to her.

To the far side, Joanne howled in pain as they wrestled her down and twisted her broken leg back into place. The sickening *crunch* of her broken bones filled the air.

The soldiers left, glad to be away from the thing in the other room.

After a few minutes, Ynya could talk once more.

"Synol, are you okay?"

Synol nodded, wordless. Tears streamed down her face. She didn't move her gaze from the doorway.

That thing had been so disgusting, so twisted.

But it had looked at Ynya with a recognition she couldn't shake.

There had been something there, something behind those eyes, an intelligence.

She searched her memory, but came up blank. She'd never seen a creature quite like that before.

But those eyes.

I've seen those eyes before, haven't I?

The night of the storm.

A chill ran up Ynya's spine at the memory. "No, it can't be."

"What?" Synol asked in a whisper.

"Gustave told me the Translator experiments on people, turning them into a new type of soldiers. I thought he meant something like the Skarmyord, human but with new abilities. I think what he really meant was whatever we just saw in there."

"What do you mean? Who was that out there? It looked kind of like a huge starving wolf but without fur."

Ynya swallowed. She wasn't sure she wanted to betray her thoughts. She didn't want Synol to have to bear the burden of that thought in her head now. But she couldn't hold back, not when it could be the truth.

"I recognize those eyes. They were same eyes I saw on Finny when we were in the eye of the storm together."

Synol gasped, her voice barely escaping her throat. "What?"

"I think that is Finny out there. I saw tubes in her arms. They must be doing something to her that is turning her into that. That must be what the Translator does."

Beside her, Synol sobbed.

"It's true," Joanne replied. Her voice was hoarse, pained, and barely above a whisper. "He's tried for years. His last one was his first successful experiment, too."

Ynya spat. "No one asked you."

"I've seen it with my own eyes. It's what they did to Firtze. He tested so high, with Ordinals all the way up his arm and onto his chest. They put him through the Enlightenments incredibly fast, like they did with me, but then the Translator took him." She coughed, a high, wheezing cough, spitting out pink foam.

Ynya recognized that sound. Joanne's lung had been punctured, and with all the blood loss from her leg, she probably wasn't long for this world.

"Firtze screamed so much. I heard him from the Pen. His screams turned into howls of pain, then just howls. They broke his mind, and his body. They turned him into something that looked like your sister out there.

"When they carted him out, a day or two before you showed up, he was locked in a metal cage. I will never forget that day. I didn't want to believe it was Firtze, but the eyes don't lie. I remember he looked at me through the bars. He knew me, but instead of smiling or waving, he growled and tried to bite through the bars."

Joanne shuddered, which turned into another violent coughing fit.

"He almost made it through, too, but they beat him into submission in front of everyone, loaded the cage onto a wagon, and left through the west gate. They took your other sister with them too."

Joanne's voice was small, barely audible. "I'm sorry, Ynya. I'm sorry I wasn't strong enough. I'm sorry I betrayed you."

Ynya growled. "It doesn't matter now. They're going to torture Tyrain over it."

There was a pause, then Joanne spoke again. "I didn't tell him where Tyrain or Aelin were."

"You what?"

"I never told them where they hid. I kept that for myself. Even through all the torture, I remembered what really mattered. Their secret is safe."

With that, Joanne devolved into another coughing fit. She let out one last wheeze and stopped.

Ynya struggled against her bonds, but wasn't able to turn enough to see Joanne's face.

"She's dead, Ynya." Synol finally said. "Joanne died."

Chapter Thirty-Nine

2201's mind whirled.

She had been trained from birth to obey the Frost Queen.

She also remembered running around in the snow, laughing and giggling. She remembered the warm embrace of a large man she called Papa, scooping her up from the snow. She remembered riding on his shoulders.

No, that is a false memory.

The Translator and the Warden huddled over her, deep in a heated conversation.

She ignored them, she had other things to think about.

Memories.

Finny was silent once again.

2201 felt her. She hadn't gone far. She stayed close at all times.

Finny had never left her because she was part of her.

She was 2201, but she was also Finny.

2201 remembered her Mama. She remembered her

Mama's sweet smile as she cleaned dirt off her face, or tucked her into bed.

Bed.

She had slept in a bed.

No! There is no sleep, only pain! There is only service to the Frost Queen!

She had slept in a bed with her sisters. They were so warm and lovely.

Ynya was the warmest.

2201 felt something new, a new type of anguish. She was sad.

Ynya wasn't warm anymore. Somehow she had her heat taken away. Something was wrong with Ynya now. She didn't have her heat. Ynya was cold. Ynya was never cold.

Ynya had magic. She had always been warm because of her magic.

Mama had magic. Mama never talked about her magic.

Finny had magic. She could control her breath and create gusts of wind to puff up Mama's skirts.

Mama taught her how to control her magic when no one else was around. It was their secret.

Her bones hardened. The serums were finishing their work. She felt the pain ebb through her veins as it finalized the changes to her body.

Finalized.

She had just come into her magic. She had just bloomed a year ago. It was before Synol left.

Synol.

Synol was next to Ynya in the other room right now. She remembered Synol had left to get married. She was so beautiful, like Mama, with long wavy hair down to her butt.

Now Synol and Ynya were in the room where the monster had been. They would become monsters soon.

Just like me. I was turned into a monster.

The howls bored into her mind. She would never forget. He had been in so much pain, even when they carted him away.

He was a monster of pain, and pain would never leave him.

She was becoming that monster of pain too, only she didn't howl.

She was stronger than him. She still had her mind.

She had Finny. Finny never left her. Finny calmed her. Finny kept her sane through all the breaking bones.

Finny *was* her.

A new pain crept into 2201, but not in her bones, nor in her head.

It was a pain in her heart.

Sadness. Loss.

She didn't want Ynya or Synol to go through the same pain she had gone through. She smelled the fear on Ynya. Ynya was afraid, afraid of never being warm again. Ynya was afraid of Finny.

She wanted Ynya to be warm again. She didn't want Ynya to be afraid of her. She remembered Ynya standing in the eye of the storm, her red hair flying wildly about her face. Ynya hadn't been afraid of her then.

Finny hadn't looked like a monster then. Finny had looked like her old self. Finny had red hair back then, before it fell out.

Before the serums took my red hair.

Her bones hardened more. She was so close. So very close to finishing her transformation. The Translator cut off his conversation with the Warden to focus on the valves and hoses going into Finny's monstrous new body.

If she finished her transformation, she would be the monster. She would never get her red hair back.

She wanted her red hair. She wanted to laugh and skip and play with her sisters again. She wanted Ynya to have her heat back. She knew Ynya missed another type of magic, a magic so incredibly powerful she could tell–

2201 recognized that magic. It was the magic of her Mama. It was the magic of Talia Oblique. She hadn't known it then, but she knew it now.

Her Mama's magic was in Ynya. She could smell it, yearning to come out and take control.

Wait.

The hardening paused for a moment before continuing.

Stop.

The hardening stopped and waited for her command.

Ynya needs to have her heat back. Synol needs to not be so sad.

She turned her head, looking around the room.

Then she saw it. She saw the thing that put the earrings in her ear. It had to be the same thing that took Ynya's magic away.

If she used it again on Ynya, she might be able to give her magic back. Ynya would be able to be warm again.

Then things would be alright.

She sat up, breaking the straps that kept her down. She realized she'd always been able to break those straps. She was strong. She was the strongest one in the room.

If she wanted to do something, she could do it.

But she didn't need to be strong. She could have her red

hair back. She liked her red hair. It was wild and crazy and fun. It made her happy.

I want my red hair back.

The serum obeyed.

Her talons disappeared into her fingers, her bones turned backwards and shrunk, making her shorter again, and her knees faced the other way.

Her mouth shrunk, and teeth retracted back into her jaw.

The men in the room yelled, but she ignored them.

They tried to grab her.

She didn't like that. She was busy right now and she didn't want to be interrupted.

The Translator grabbed her shoulder. "What are you doing? The transformation isn't complete!"

She spun, looking into his eyes. He was afraid. She smelled the fear on both men.

The Translator was afraid, but the Warden was the most afraid.

She reached up with her smooth-skinned hand and grabbed the Translator's wrist. She twisted his arm until it snapped.

"You will not touch me again."

His eyes went wide as he screamed.

She turned her head slightly to the side, studying him. "Why do you cry? I thought pain was a good thing? Isn't that what you told me when I was in pain? Isn't that what you told me when I asked for just one second without the pain?"

The Warden turned to run, but she didn't want him to run. He had also caused her pain.

She used her wind to grab him and throw him into the wall, pinning him there.

The Translator fell to his knees, still screaming. "2201, stop this at once!"

"2201?" She pursed her lips, remembering. "That's not correct. My name is Finny Oblique, and I'm going to give my sister back her magic."

Finny picked up the apparatus off the table and turned it over in her hands. She remembered when she first came to this prison that they had used this on her.

Her hand went up to her ear, feeling for the spot where they had punctured her. She felt the hole, but she didn't like the hole.

She told the serum to close off the hole. She wanted smooth skin.

The serum complied.

Finny walked into the side room and looked at Ynya.

Ynya cried. She also smiled. She cried while smiling. That was odd.

"Hello, Ynya. Finny is sad that you aren't warm. Do you want to be warm?"

Ynya nodded. "Yes, Finny. I would like to be warm again."

Chapter Forty

Ynya had been so long without her inner fire that when Finny removed the earring with the tool, the surge of heat overwhelmed Ynya's frail body.

She convulsed as the magic surged through her. It latched onto her spine, running down her nerves and veins, and poured into her extremities.

The magic filled her head, propelled out of her skull and into her hair. The room lit as her hair heated, filling every corner with a blinding light.

Finny cut her from the table, but Ynya didn't move. She needed to feel the burn in her again, she wanted to relish it.

A voice she hadn't heard inside her told her she had no time left.

She needed to act.

Synol cried beside her.

Ynya felt the tidal rush of magic as her older sister regained her magic once again.

Ynya fell off the table and onto the floor.

She huddled there for a long moment, regaining her

strength. The heat warmed deep inside, rousing the inner-most parts of her soul.

A shiver ran up her spine, and she stood.

She was back.

Finny looked at her with a curious expression.

"Finny, you have grown."

Finny looked like herself once again, but she was taller, now. In fact, she was so large that she was bigger than Synol.

Finny's unblinking gaze bored into her for a long moment before flicking away. "Yes, I am larger now. I want to be big. I do not want to be small anymore."

Ynya looked up at her, not quite sure how to process the fact that her little sister now towered over her by half a foot.

"As long as it makes you happy." Ynya held out her hand. "May I have the tool and the earrings? I want to give a present to our hosts."

Finny deposited the objects into her hand.

Ynya weighed the items in her palm. It was terrifying that such a small hoop of metal could have such a profound impact on her ability to cast her magic. She stared at it for a while, her mind ruminating on her life without magic. She'd been help-less in some ways, but it had also forced her to learn to cope without her inner fire.

She wasn't sure what to think about having her magic back again. Magic had been such a part of her that she hadn't real-ized what life was truly like for those that didn't have magic. Here she stood in an entire place that thrived on the fact that some people had magic, and others didn't.

Magic was taken away from those deemed unworthy, and given to those who were. The entire prison existed purely to keep those with magic in line.

Ynya shuddered. It was all too much to take in right now. She should just be glad she had her magic back.

Beside her, Synol stood on shaky legs.

"How do you feel, Syni?"

She poked her stomach and legs with a finger. "I think I'm alright."

Synol looked up at Finny, who was now an inch taller than her. "I missed you, Finny." Her eyes filled with tears and she twitched her hands. "Are...are you alright?"

Finny looked at Synol with the same curious expression. "I am."

Synol's voice broke and she threw herself at her little sister, pulling her into an embrace like her life depended on it.

Ynya's heart melted at the sight and she took a step closer to join her sisters.

Finny opened up her other arm and pulled both sisters close. "I'm not the same anymore, sisters."

Synol's voice was muffed, being buried in Finny's shoulder. "I don't think any of us are the same anymore, Fin. But we're together, and that's all that matters."

Chapter Forty-One

Finny broke the embrace and thrust out her hand. In the other room, a man's voice cried out. There was a crack of bone and a grunt.

"What was that?"

"He tried to run."

Synol and Ynya shared a look.

The three sisters walked into the other room. Wind magic held the Warden against the wall, unable to move.

The Translator lay on the ground, his head snapped and facing behind him.

"Why did you kill him?"

Finny turned to look at Ynya. "He has spent multiple generations torturing kids and turning them into monsters. There is no redemption for him."

The Warden's steely gaze focused on Ynya, the malice palpable in his eyes. "She's right, you know. You might as well do the same to me."

Ynya took the silver dagger from the Warden's sheath and tossed it the other side of the room.

"I remember you said something to me, Warden, something about obeying, and something about being fast. Do you remember that? It's been so long and we've had so many good conversations since then, that I just don't remember exactly what was said."

Ynya put the brass earring in his ear, locking it in with the earring tool. She poured heat into the earring machine, melting it in front of him, dripping hot metal on the floor.

Ynya turned to her sister. "It's okay, Finny, you can let him go now."

Finny turned off the wind that held the man to the wall.

The Warden's gaze never left Finny's. "Why don't you just kill me like you did him?"

Ynya folded her arms and stared at the man. "It's tempting, but we're going to try to end this peacefully rather than with violence."

The Warden smiled. "But you are a creature of violence, my dear Ynya. All three of you have blood on your hands that will never wash off. Like it or not, but you're a part of my world, more so than you would like to admit."

"That may be, but we're going to at least give them the choice, which is more than you gave any of us."

THE THREE GIRLS EXITED THE WHITE BUILDING TO THE stares of the entire camp.

Ynya threw the captured Warden to the ground.

"I want everyone to pay attention!" Ynya yelled with the aid of Finny's air magic, projecting her voice much farther than she normally could by herself. "We have taken over

Reyoarfjell. It no longer belongs to the Frost Queen, and our dear Warden here has been dethroned."

Ynya nudged the man with her foot, rolling him over.

"All prisoners will be released immediately. Any that are able, we ask that you find food and clothes for the remaining prisoners to help get them healthy for their travels back home. We will be organizing everyone into traveling parties."

From the side, two soldiers drew swords and came at the sisters.

Two small cyclones materialized and picked up both men, tossing them a dozen feet into the air. Both came down to the earth with a sickening *crunch*.

"Any other soldiers who disagree with the sudden change in management are welcome to air their grievances with my little sister here. Meanwhile, we're going to need some volunteers to help organize everyone into parties to search this place for all its valuables."

Ynya paused to let her announcement sink in, then spoke again to everyone in the Pit. "You're all going home."

"Ynya, we are ready."

Ynya closed her right hand and stood up from the desk. "I'll be right there."

Synol stared curiously at her from the doorway. "Find anything good in the Warden's desk?"

Ynya held up the book with her left hand. "Just the ledger with Mama's name in it."

"Were you going to add it to the others?"

Ynya nodded. "Yes. It should go with all the other records. Is Gustave still willing to take it all back to Marsfjord?"

Synol nodded, but pursed her lips. "Did you find any other information in it?"

Ynya chuckled. "You mean the part where Mama had three siblings who all were here, or the part where she was here sixty years ago?"

Ynya dropped the ledger on the table and slid it across the desk. "I don't know what to think about any of it anymore. I feel like we don't know much about her. Mostly I just want to know why the Warden has this one ledger in his personal desk when there is a hall of records."

Synol took a couple steps into the room and picked up the ledger. She frowned as she thumbed through the pages. "Perhaps the only answers we're going to get are ones we don't want to hear. Maybe we won't like the answers regardless of the truth."

Ynya let out a slow breath. "Let's finish destroying this place and go get Meki. The longer we stay around here, the more I question my sanity."

"I'll get this to Gustave. You're going to come see him off?"

Ynya nodded, a small smile gracing her lips for the first time in a day. She hoped Synol didn't notice. To cover, she said, "Thank you, Synol. Thank you for handling all of this."

It was Synol's turn to chuckle. "I like helping people. Doing this helps me feel like I have a purpose."

AFTER ALL THE PEOPLE HAD BEEN RESCUED, THE PLACE ransacked, and a dozen wagons loaded up with refugees from the camp left for their respective homes, the storm raged through the camp once again. This time, it left no stone untouched, no piece of metal unburied.

Over the course of an entire day, Synol and Finny destroyed and buried Reyoarfjell, eradicating it from the land. Wind and earth worked together for the destruction of a place that had brought so much pain and suffering to everyone.

It was a bittersweet moment for Ynya. She was glad it was gone, but she wondered if leaving it here abandoned, allowing nature to overtake it, was the better choice. It wasn't really the fault of the buildings, and part of her hoped that leaving it would be a reminder to future generations of the atrocities that had gone on here.

While her sisters buried the compound, Ynya pulled something from her pocket. Deep inside the Warden's personal desk, she had found a single gold earring. Ynya felt the unique thrum of magic through it.

The Warden had smiled broadly when she inquired about it, telling her to try it on, just for a second. She hadn't, but she got the feeling that it might be useful one day.

She pocketed it, then made sure the single bronze and single silver earring still remained hidden in her bag. She didn't want to tell her sisters that she dreamed of the day when she would be able to put them in her own ear and live like a normal human, without the threat of magic torturing her soul.

Epilogue

Imryll Farora watched as Captain Nora Oblique returned to the front gate of Fellsstrond Castle. She noted the extra rider and wagon following a ways behind.

"Khatar, I think we should prepare for some guests, what do you say?"

"I think that is a wonderful idea, My Lady. I shall have the kitchen bring up some food immediately. Anything special you wish?"

Imryll thought for a moment. "Hot chocolate. I think my guest will appreciate the extra sweetness."

"As you wish, My Lady."

Khatar disappeared and in less than a minute, servants buzzed about the room preparing tables and chairs. Placemats were set and shiny silver goblets glimmered in the firelight.

In ten short minutes, the whole room smelled of roasted pig, the kitchen always keeping one on slow roast just in case the need ever came up.

"Mmm. I especially love this mulled wine."

Before she finished half a goblet, the servants had set the

table, prepared all the food, and vanished without a trace, leaving Khatar dressed in his finest.

Imryll sipped more of the mulled wine, wondering if it tasted better hot, like it had been prepared this time.

Khatar cleared his throat and walked toward the entry door.

A second later, a knock came.

"Come in."

Captain Nora came through, bowing.

"I returned as you asked, My Lady, and I brought what you desired."

Behind her, a young girl with bright red hair stood. In her hands she held a small stuffed bear.

Imryll stood, and walked across the floor, her shoes clacking with each step.

"I see that, but I fail to see the second that I had requested."

Nora tensed. "My Lady, the Translator took the other one for one of his experiments, swapping her out with a fool who ended up freezing to death on the way here."

"I see," Imryll said, tapping her long blue fingernails on her chin. "I did notice you came in with a wagon?"

Nora nodded, keeping her eyes still down at the stone floor. "The Translator sent along a...creature, My Lady. He says it's the first of its kind. He said it was a present for you, after all the years of work. He apologized for not returning the other girl, but promised she would be an even more spectacular specimen now that he knew how to keep their bodies from breaking."

Imryll chuckled. "Well, I can't very well blame you for not returning with what I asked for when you aren't provided it by my other servants, can I?"

Wisely, Nora didn't reply.

"You may go, I wish to dine with this young one for now."

Nora turned to leave.

Imryll knelt down, coming eye to eye with the little red-haired girl. "Hello there. My name is Imryll. What is your name?"

The little girl didn't reply, instead looking around the large room.

"Come in, my dear. There is no need to be afraid. Do you want some hot chocolate?"

Imryll put out her hand.

The little girl looked at her for a second, but finally put out her little hand.

Imryll led the girl to the bench and helped her up, finally easing into her spot at the head of the table. She picked up her mulled wine once again and sipped it.

Yes, hot is better.

"So, please dear, what is your name?"

"Meki."

"Meki? That is a fine name, don't you think, Khatar?"

"Yes, My Lady, quite a fine name for a fine young lady."

Imryll leaned forward, lowering her voice at the young girl. "Well, Meki, I'm so very glad you have come to join me here at my castle. You are my guest, and as my guest you will be treated like royalty, not like that vile woman who brought you here."

Meki looked around. "Will I have to be near that monster?"

"Oh, no. Not at all. That thing will stay downstairs, where it belongs."

"Good, I don't like that thing. I also want to see my sisters."

Imryll sipped her wine once again. "I understand that, but

I cannot command them to come here. They will have to make it here on their own."

"I think they will come find me."

Imryll smiled as she put down her wine goblet. She picked up a small cookie and rolled it around on her finger. "Oh, I think they will come to find you, my dear. I'm counting on it."

THE END

I HOPE YOU ENJOYED THIS BOOK! IF YOU DID, PLEASE leave a review on Amazon or Goodreads. Reviews help others find my books, which means I can continue to write more like this!

Thank you so much for reading, and I hope you check out the next episode in The Frost Fervor Concordance!

- Tom Hansen

November 2018

Author's Notes

November 2018

I took a serious leap of faith with this book.

Just like the last book, I wrote this book in just over three weeks. I took one week off in the middle to go to Vegas for the best writer's conference there is.

So it really took me two and a half, but who's counting.

I knew before I even wrote book one what the general plot would be for this book. *Concentration Camp*. I knew I wanted the evil guys running experiments on the prisoners. I also knew that Finny would be here, but Meki wouldn't. Past that detail, I didn't know much else of what I was putting into this story.

Shortly after I started, I had to go to a writer's conference in Vegas, as mentioned earlier. Well, as much as I had hoped, I never get enough writing done while AT the conferences, mostly because I'm spending my day in classes, meeting new people, catching up with old friends, passing out business cards, and eating.

Lots of eating.

Unfortunately the calories don't get the message that they were supposed to stay in Vegas.

But while I was there, I got inspired by one of the talks and decided to tweak my writing method slightly for this book.

Okay, I'll admit it, I was completely stuck.

I managed to get Ynya and Synol into the camp, and got them captured, but then I didn't know what to do with them once they got the earrings in their ears. I had written myself two powerful mages, who couldn't use their magic.

To be honest, I thought about turning to The Great Escape for inspiration, or any one of the prison escape stories out there, but then I realized I had someone else I could use. Someone who still had magic and would be able to cause enough disruption to the camp to allow my non-magic heroes some wiggle room.

I had Finny.

And thus, I finished the book.

Once I figured out that one bit, the rest was easy. Or, well, easier, because I had to fix some of the earlier things to make it match, but that's what editing is for. Writing something brilliant near the end of the book means you now have to go back and change the rest of the story to match.

Anyway, I hope you enjoy reading this book as much as I did writing it! I still tried to hit the same beats in this as I did with the last one. Sisterly love, pain, friendship, reliance on others, standing up against evil, saving someone from a fate worse than death. It's all here.

If you loved this book, I think you'll love the next one. Blazing Vengeance is out now and you can read an excerpt on the next page!

One of the best ways to support me as an author is to leave

a review on Amazon. Reviews help others find my books, which means I can continue to write more like this!

I realize Amazon doesn't make it easy to leave a review because you can't just hit stars and move on, but even a simple review like "Sistas 4 Lyfe!" goes a long to letting others know that this series is worth checking out.

Sharing the book with others on social media helps get the word out. So hop on the Twitters and the Instagrams. Shout from the top of the Facebooks and the Reddits that you love my story!

While you're there, come say hi! I love to hear how my stories have entertained or touched you.

Finally, I have so many other stories to tell in this universe, and I've already written one that I want to share with you. Consider signing up to my newsletter so you can be notified of future releases!

Thank you so much for reading, and I'll see you next time!

- Tom Hansen

November 2018

Excerpt from Blazing Vengeance

BOOK THREE OF THE FROST FERVOR
CONCORDANCE

Ynya Oblique ground her teeth as Synol said her goodbyes for the ninth time.

"You shouldn't do that. You can't regenerate your teeth." Finny said in her matter-of-fact manner.

Ynya rolled her eyes. "I'm well aware that I shouldn't do it, I just don't care. I want Synol to hurry up."

"Then why don't you just tell her that?"

Ynya looked over at her sister. In the four weeks they'd been traveling together, Ynya still had a hard time knowing if Finny was making a joke or not.

Finny had always been a very literal girl, and it was cute when she was younger. But whatever torture they did to her as part of the Enlightenments back at Reyoarfjell had changed her into something Ynya wasn't quite sure how to handle.

Finny's mind wasn't the same that had entered that facility weeks ago. Sometimes she was caring and warm, other times she was cold and literal to a fault. Others, she was brimming with rage and pain and refused to talk to anyone.

The last one was the one Ynya worried about most. She

knew the rage, she had spent her whole life bathed in its fiery heat, but she had changed in the last few months. She was at war, and war changed you. Sometimes you had to make tough choices in order to squeak by. Loss and anguish seemed to follow her everywhere she went now. No matter what choice you make, someone ended up getting hurt, and Ynya wasn't sure she could live with the consequences of her decisions.

When she had first found her parents slaughtered, she had made a choice of who of her sisters to rescue first. Ultimately, she had rescued Synol, and Ynya wondered if she shouldn't have just continued her pursuit after her two younger ones instead. Yes, Synol needed saving from her horrible husband, but the cost to Finny's mind and body had been great.

Ynya looked her sister. Despite being four years younger, Finny was now as large as Synol, without the mature features you normally got with age. Ynya wondered if Finny would continue to grow as she aged. It was something Finny had decided to do when she transformed from the beast on the table back to her human form.

Ynya pursed her lips and nodded at Synol. "It's the polite thing to do, to allow her to say goodbye in the manner she prefers."

"But she is frustrating you and you should tell her so she stops."

"If I just grabbed her and pulled her away, then she and I would have a fight." Ynya grabbed the bridge of her nose and squeezed. It was an action she'd seen her mother do a thousand times growing up, as she tried to keep her own anger down and not yell at her petulant little fire-headed daughters.

"Any frustration I feel is my own, it's all in my head. Just because she might be doing something that bothers me does't mean it's her fault. Does that make sense? I'm the one *choosing* to be irritated. Synol isn't doing it on purpose to, and if I drag her into my own problems, then I have just spread my own toxicity to others."

Ynya paused, realizing she sounded just like her mother. *Ugh!*

In fact she was pretty sure that was an exact Talia Oblique quote.

"The point is, she's not *being* irritating, I'm the one *getting* irritated. It's my problem and not worth a fight with Synol." A small smirk crossed her lips as she pulled a small vial from her belt. "Though that won't stop me from dumping some fire ants into her bedroll tonight."

Finny looked at the vial for a second before a broad smile crossed her lips. She let out a loud guffaw. "Oh that will be so funny watching her crying from all the bites on her legs!"

Ynya put the vial away as Synol turned in their direction. "Well, I can't do it now, because you just gave it away."

Finny stopped laughing. "I'm sorry. I didn't realize how loud I was just now."

Ynya patted her sister's arm. "It's fine, but I think that gave us our exit finally."

Synol joined them a few seconds later. "I'm sorry, I didn't realize I had kept gossiping so long. What was that about bites on legs?"

Ynya glanced at Finny, who's eyes were bright with pleading mischief. Ynya shook her head slightly. "Oh, nothing. So how are they?"

Synol frowned. "They are more worried than they let on. It's dangerous for them to put us up for so long this close to the Frost Queen's lair. Her family would have serious ramifications if word got out."

"We kept our hair covered the whole time we were here, I don't think anyone noticed."

Synol frowned again. "I'm not sure that is enough. Three girls traveling through by themselves this close to Fellsstrond Castle is enough to raise a few eyebrows, let alone the fact that there is basically no one in the Skarfanes that isn't wearing a uniform."

Rather than replying, Ynya kept marching.

Finally, Synol stopped them and pulled Ynya into a big bear hug. "Thank you for waiting patiently, I just had such a hard time leaving them knowing that I probably sentenced them to death for their hospitality. I know you wanted to be there by now, but I just–"

Ynya hugged back. "Take the time that you need, Synol. I know how much it means to you. We will get there when we get there. Besides, it's not like hugging the people who gave us a warm bed is the only thing keeping us from getting there."

Ynya, despite her trepidation at how long it was taking to cross the Skarfanes, knew this was going to take time. They had been in enemy territory for weeks now, and every step they made needed to be planned carefully.

Too much rode on their caution, and balancing that with speed was just one of the many things that kept her up at night.

Who knew what the Frost Queen was doing to her sister at this very moment. After seeing the atrocities they did to the prisoners in Reyoarfjell, Ynya had a terrifying new understanding of human nature.

And she wasn't sure she liked being part of the populous anymore.

How one person could do those things to another was beyond her. Killing, she understood. Sometimes it was needed, sometimes there was no other choice. If one is forced to kill, at least do it humanely, quickly. End their life with the least amount of suffering.

But torture, and the dastardly games The Warden did to his victims, that was just suffering for suffering's sake.

No amount of suffering validates the end result. You can't justify violence against someone unless you are saving your life or the life of someone else.

You just can't.

"Ynya?" Synol frowned at her. "You okay?"

Ynya nodded. "Yeah. Sorry, I'm just tired is all."

While that statement was true, it wasn't the only reason she had been in her head so much lately. The reality of why Ynya hadn't been getting after Synol to hurry up and get Meki back was that Ynya was terrified of what she would have to do once she got there.

So far, they had avoided most of the patrols, and only had to take out the occasional soldier who discovered them.

But Synol or Finny had done all those killings.

Ynya had allowed them.

She didn't know if she could kill again. She didn't know if she could justify it in the name of her safety.

Ynya shuddered with the thought. Reyoarfjell had clearly changed her outlook on life.

She had changed more than she thought in the last couple months, and it terrified her to realize it.

She reached into the pocket containing the magic-preventing earrings she had saved from being buried with Reyoarfjell when it was torn down.

Part of her knew they might come in handy.

Check out Blazing Vengeance: Book Three in the Frost Fervor Concordance now!

About Tom Hansen

THE CREATIVE CURMUDGEON

FANTASTIC WORLDS. GET-OFF-MY-LAWN ATTITUDE.

Tom Hansen is the writer and lover of all things fantasy. While he can't seem to stick to a specific genre, you can rest assured that anything he writes will have that aspect of whimsy and world building that defines the fantasy genre.

His first series is the *End Gate Chronicles*, a modern-day urban fantasy following an older widow who discovers her own magic late in life.

His second series, *Enter the louVRe*, is set inside a video game, where an evil AI has trapped players and stolen their memories. Now, a lone minotaur must save the world from destruction if he has any hope to to unravel the plans of the architect of the game and escape unscathed.

His third series, *The Frost Fervor Concordance*, is set in a fantastical frozen wasteland, where a young fisher comes home to find her village burned and her parents killed. The fire-headed mage must track down her kidnapped sisters and battle the Frost Queen's tyranny in order to keep her sisters safe.

Tom lives in Arizona with his dear wife, four children, and two cats.

To follow Tom, check out his website or any of the link below:
www.scarhoof.com

facebook.com/scarhoof

twitter.com/scarhoof

amazon.com/author/tomhansen

bookbub.com/authors/tom-hansen-7a3f964c-dbe3-4b40-a702-f7c60c91c3b3

goodreads.com/scarhoof

youtube.com/scarhoofplays

instagram.com/Scarhoof

Also by Tom Hansen

WWW.SCARHOOF.COM/ALSOBYTOMHANSEN

Adventure Fantasy

THE FROST FERVOR CONCORDANCE:

Inciting Vengeance (Prequel - Coming Spring 2019)

Igniting Vengeance

Flaming Vengeance

Blazing Vengeance

The Frost Fervor Concordance Trilogy (Books 1-3 plus bonus Novella! - Coming Spring 2019)

Sparking Vengeance (Coming Mid 2019)

Flaring Vengeance (Coming Mid 2019)

LitRPG/GameLit

ENTER THE louVRe SERIES:

Eloria's Beginning

Eloria's Calling (Coming 2019)

BECOMING DEATH SERIES:

Mightier Still

Urban Fantasy

END GATE SERIES:

A Moonlit Task

Mayhem in the Moonlight (Coming Early 2019)

Secrets of the Shadowed Moon (Coming Early 2019)

THE KORRIGAN CHRONICLES:

The Sacking of Gildebrand Manor

That Dammed Berehynia

Moloch's Twisted Menagerie

Freya's Wild Hunt

The Roswell Incident

Short Fiction/Anthologies

Ynya vs the Frost Bear: A Frost Fervor Concordance Prequel Short

Into the Void: A Steampunk Short Story

Glimpses: an Anthology of 16 Short Fantasy Stories

Futurism & Fantasia: Volume 1: First Chapters

Newsletter Exclusives

Miss-Miss's Near Miss (Adventure Fantasy)

Splashes of Wine (Urban Fantasy)

The Curious Case of Brendalynn Bobbins (LitRPG)

.

www.ingramcontent.com/pod-product-compliance
Lightning Source LLC
Chambersburg PA
CBHW020944180626
46814CB00003B/928